IT TAKES TWO

'Tis the Off-Season

by Belle Payton

Simon Spotlight

New York   London   Toronto   Sydney   New Delhi

SIMON SPOTLIGHT
An imprint of Simon & Schuster Children's Publishing Division
1230 Avenue of the Americas, New York, New York 10020
This Simon Spotlight edition November 2015
© 2015 by Simon & Schuster, Inc.
All rights reserved, including the right of reproduction in whole or in part in any form.
SIMON SPOTLIGHT and colophon are registered trademarks of
Simon & Schuster, Inc.
Text by Sarah Albee
Cover art by Anthony VanArsdale
For information about special discounts for bulk purchases, please
contact Simon & Schuster Special Sales at 1-866-506-1949 or
business@simonandschuster.com.
Designed by Ciara Gay
The text of this book was set in Garamond.
Manufactured in the United States of America 1015 FFG
10 9 8 7 6 5 4 3 2 1
ISBN 978-1-4814-4206-0 (hc)
ISBN 978-1-4814-4205-3 (pbk)
ISBN 978-1-4814-4207-7 (eBook)
Library of Congress Catalog Card Number 2014952442

CHAPTER ONE

"How about this one?" Alex Sackett asked. She twirled around so that her twin sister, Ava, could admire the way her pleated green skirt flared. "Do you think it's festive enough for a party?"

Ava was lying on the kitchen floor alongside their dog, Moxy, rubbing Moxy's furry stomach. She and Moxy both looked up. Ava cocked her head sideways as she regarded her twin. "I guess so," she said. "But Al, Christmas is three weeks away. I've barely recovered from Thanksgiving. What party are you even talking about?"

Alex pursed her lips and gazed at her own reflection in the kitchen window. Now that it was December, darkness fell early. She smoothed her hair. "I haven't been invited to any parties yet, but there will very likely be quite a few, given this town's penchant for celebration."

Ava grinned. Her sister had probably been itching to use the word "penchant" in a sentence. Ava had borrowed a pencil off Alex's desk that morning—they were always sharp, with good erasers—so she knew that Alex was still going strong with her stack of SAT vocabulary cards. Moxy rolled onto her back, all four paws straight in the air, to give Ava better access to tummy rubbing.

"And I'm bound to be invited, being that I'm seventh-grade class president and all."

"Oh, yes, I almost forgot about that," said Ava drily.

Alex didn't seem to hear the sarcasm in Ava's tone. "And as president, I really think people look to me for style tips," she continued.

Alex moved to a cupboard door that Ava had left open, and closed it with exaggerated annoyance. "Still, I'm finding it a challenge to dress for the Christmas holiday season in a place where it never snows. I may not even have a chance to wear those boots I bought at the end-of-season sale last winter back in Massachusetts. That would be totally tragic." The Sacketts had moved from Massachusetts to Texas just this past July. The twins were still getting used to the fact that it didn't snow—or get very cold at all—in their new town.

"I wouldn't be so sure about that, honey." Their father, Coach Mike Sackett, loomed in the kitchen doorway. "Ashland does see snow from time to time. Maybe not as much as Massachusetts, but that's fine with me. I'm not going to miss shoveling the driveway in February."

Moxy scrambled to her feet and charged over to Coach, wagging her whole back end with delight. He reached down and fluffed the dog's ears. His hair was damp and combed and Ava noticed a dab of shaving cream just below his chin. She felt a surge of affection for her dad. He was the head coach of the Ashland Tigers football team—that was the reason they'd moved. It was a high-pressure job, but a few weeks ago Coach had shown the town he had what it took to win the state championship in his very first season.

"At least I'll be able to wear my new boots when we go to Massachusetts for Christmas," said Alex.

Ava shook her head as she got to her feet. Her sister was a planner. Alex was the sort of person who bought Christmas presents for people in July, when she saw "just the right thing."

"Hey, Coach," said Ava. "Who's going to look after Moxy when we're in Massachusetts?"

"What?" Coach glanced down at Moxy with a startled look, as though he'd forgotten she existed. Moxy, annoyed that he'd stopped petting her ears, pawed his pant leg. "Oh, uh, we'll work all that out," he said. He seemed relieved when Mrs. Sackett bustled into the kitchen, fastening her earring.

She had put on a black dress and was holding a pair of strappy shoes, but Ava could see a streak of blue paint on her wrist. She grinned. Her mom might look put-together at first glance, but the twins could always spot some evidence of her artsy side.

"Girls, are you sure you're okay making your own dinner tonight?" she asked them, hopping a little as she slipped first one foot and then the other into her shoes. "Tommy's going out with Cassie, so it's just you two."

"Of course we're sure," both girls said at the same time. Ava was glad her brother wasn't here.

She and Alex often said the same thing, or finished each other's sentences, and Tommy called it their creepy twin thing. It was something they'd been doing ever since they had both learned to talk.

"You and Daddy have fun. Ave and I are going to watch a romantic movie," said Alex.

Ava smiled and nodded at their mom. In fact, the idea of sending their parents on a date tonight had been her idea. Football season was over for all of them—not just for Coach, but for Tommy, too, who was a sophomore and a player on the team, and also for Ava, who was the only girl on the Ashland Middle School team. But the real reason Ava had proposed that her parents go out tonight was because she wanted to distract them from asking how her math test had gone today. (Answer: not too well.)

Tommy barged in, engulfed in a cloud of body spray. He stepped around Moxy and opened the refrigerator door to peer inside.

"Why are you eating now? Aren't you and Cassie going out for pizza tonight?" asked Alex.

"Yep," said Tommy, pulling out the fixings to make himself a sandwich. "That's why I need to pre-eat. I can't show her my fearsome appetite this early in our relationship or I might scare her off."

"And, let me guess, you're planning to pay, too, right?" asked Ava with a sly look. "You can't eat as much as you would if Mom and Dad were footing the bill."

"Now, Ave," said Mrs. Sackett, suppressing a smile.

"You ready, honey?" Coach asked their mom, picking up the car keys.

Mrs. Sackett nodded as Coach opened the kitchen door and stepped aside to let her pass.

"I can't believe we're going on an actual date on an actual Friday night," she said with a laugh. "And that we don't have to watch a football film tonight."

"I never said that," said Coach with a grin. "The night is young."

"He's so romantic," sighed Mrs. Sackett.

Alex followed them to the door and waved as they drove away. A few minutes later, Tommy polished off the last bite of his sandwich and then he, too, left. And then it was just the two of them and Moxy.

"Yes!" said Ava. She pulled the jar of popcorn kernels and a bottle of oil out of a cupboard.

"Mom forgot all about my math test." She put her ten fingertips together, wiggling them evil-villain-style, and pretended to cackle. "My little scheme worked out perfectly!" she said.

Alex crossed her arms and gazed sternly at her sister. "Did you seriously concoct this date idea for Mom and Dad so they wouldn't ask you about the math test you took today?"

Ava smiled sweetly. "I might have."

"That is so pernicious of you!" said Alex. Another vocab word.

"I just didn't feel like thinking about school-work on a Friday night," said Ava. "Plus I have the whole weekend to do homework. I don't have a game tomorrow, remember? I've got nothing but time on my hands until basketball season starts, and that won't be until after Christmas break." As the athletic half of the twins, not only had Ava been the lone girl on the football team, but she was planning to try out for the basketball team for the winter season. Luckily, there was a girls' team, so Ava wouldn't have to deal with all the publicity she'd had to endure during the football season.

Her sister dropped the stern face and moved to pull a big mixing bowl out of the bottom cupboard. "You make the popcorn. I'll get started on the chocolate chip cookies."

"Sounds good," agreed Ava. "And it's my turn to pick the movie, so forget romance—let's watch something scary!"

Half an hour later, the cookies were in the oven and the two sisters were settled in on opposite ends of the comfy couch in Coach's study, watching the opening credits of a new thriller they'd both wanted to see. Moxy lay between them, snoring gently. Moxy was not permitted on the couch when their mom was home, but she took every opportunity she could get to jump up when Mrs. Sackett was out. Each girl cradled a big bowl of buttered popcorn.

Just five minutes into the movie, Moxy lifted her head, her eyes wide open, her ears cocked expectantly. She leaped down from the couch and began barking her head off.

"Did someone knock?" Alex asked Ava.

Ava paused the movie. "I'm not sure."

Alex slipped her feet into her fluffy pink bunny slippers and then shuffled out of the room toward the front door. She peered through the peephole. Moxy was still barking.

Ava stood up too and watched at the door of

the study as her sister jerked her face away from the peephole and gasped. She turned and stared at Ava, her green eyes round with surprise.

"It's Corey!" she mouthed silently.

Corey O'Sullivan? What was he doing here on a Friday night?

Alex became a panicked mess. She kicked off her bunny slippers and threw them behind the umbrella stand. She pulled out her hair tie and frantically fluffed her hair into place. "Why is he here?" she whispered to Ava. "How does my hair look? Of all the times to be wearing this shirt!" She stared down at her old, comfy T-shirt with the purple sparkly unicorn on it.

Ava rolled her eyes, moved her sister gently out of the way, and opened the door.

"Hey, Ave," said Corey. He seemed relieved to see her. Corey was the quarterback of the middle school football team, and he and Ava had gotten pretty close during the season. Then he noticed Alex standing behind Ava, and suddenly his gaze dropped and he stared to the left and to the right and then down at his sneakers.

"Hey, Corey," said Ava. "What's up? Do you want to come in? We're watching *Don't Look*, but it just started."

"What? No. I mean, thanks, no. I just had a, um, a, um, a question," said Corey, his voice barely audible.

This was so weird. *Why is he so nervous?* Ava wondered.

"Hi!" squeaked Alex. She stepped out from where she'd been hiding behind Ava.

Corey's gaze flicked up to Alex and then quickly away. "Oh, hey, Alex. Didn't expect to find you here."

"Why not?" demanded Ava. "She lives here."

"Oh, ha-ha, yeah, that's right," said Corey.

"Ha-ha," agreed Alex.

"Ha-ha," said Corey.

The conversation lagged. Corey took off his baseball cap, scratched behind his ear, and put it back on.

"So do you want to come in?" asked Ava, starting to feel exasperated.

"No! I mean, um, no, thanks. I just wanted to ask Alex something quickly," said Corey.

Ava raised her eyebrows. Alex nodded expectantly.

"I just wanted to ask . . . ," he said.

The twins waited.

". . . to ask . . ."

Moxy, who had stopped barking when she saw it was Corey, poked her head out and sniffed in Corey's direction, then wagged her tail encouragingly.

". . . to ask what the math homework is!" he finally blurted out.

Alex blinked. "Oh! Ah, the *math* homework? Um, let me think."

There was an awkward pause, and Corey seemed to be looking around for help.

"Oh, right," said Alex. "Officially we don't have any, unless you want to start reviewing for the quiz on unit three, which is going to be on Tuesday," she said, her voice slightly higher than usual. Ava knew Alex always got nervous talking to boys. "I might do a few practice problems," added Alex, " because quadratic equations can be tricky."

Ava rolled her eyes. Alex was brilliant at quadratic equations. But Ava knew she would do more than "a few" practice problems anyway.

"Got it. Thanks," said Corey. "Well, see you guys." He darted down the front steps toward his bike, which was lying on its side on the front lawn.

"Bye!" the girls called after him. They watched

him put on the reflective vest that all the kids in the neighborhood wore when they rode their bikes at night. Corey didn't live very far away, but he must have *really* wanted to know about the math homework.

Ava pulled Alex away from the door and then shut and locked it again. "Well, that was random," she said. "Come on. Let's get back to the movie."

But Alex had moved to the little window next to the door so she could watch Corey pedal away.

"Why do you think he came here to ask me about homework on a Friday night?" she asked. "Why didn't he just text me?"

Ava shrugged. "Beats me. Maybe he wanted to get in some cardio. Come on."

"I mean, he and Lindsey are definitely broken up, so it's okay that he showed up at our house, right? Do you think he might like me?"

Ava sighed. "Al, I don't know. I don't have that kind of relationship with Corey. We're teammates. I stay out of that stuff."

"Well, this has the potential to get complicated with Lindsey," said Alex, slowly following her sister back to the study. "I finally feel like

Lindsey and I are becoming good friends. What would she think if Corey and I started liking each other? I mean, how can I not interpret this sudden visit from Corey as an indication that he might like me?"

Ava sniffed. "Uh-oh," she said. "I think we have bigger problems to worry about right now than whether Corey likes you."

Alex had smelled it too. "The cookies!" she shrieked, and raced to the kitchen.

CHAPTER TWO

"Ave, it's not going to fit. Trust me," said Alex. It was Monday morning, and she and Ava were at their lockers. Ava was trying to cram her basketball into the bottom part of her locker. "It's a sphere," Alex pointed out as kindly as she could. "Which means no matter how you turn it, it's going to be the same shape."

"Well, it needs air," said Ava, slightly defensively. "I thought I could get it in if I squeezed it a little, but I guess that's not happening. Oh well. I'll just carry it around."

"You'd better not dribble it inside this building," said Alex. "Or Ms. Farmen will have your head."

Ava had been driving Alex crazy recently, dribbling the basketball everywhere she went, including inside the house. She was working on improving her ball-handling skills.

"I've been thinking nonstop about Lindsey and Corey," said Alex, as she folded her purple cardigan into a neat square and placed it on the upper shelf of her locker.

"I know. You've been *talking* nonstop about Lindsey and Corey too," said Ava.

Alex slipped her math book onto the neat stack of books and pulled out her social studies book. Out of the corner of her eye, she saw her sister shove a book into the crowded locker and slam it shut before the towering stack could fall out. "I want to ask Emily if she thinks Lindsey would get mad if Corey and I liked each other."

Ava held her locker door closed with her hip while she gave her combination a spin. The door didn't burst back open, and she nodded, satisfied.

"Ava!"

Callie Wagner rushed up to them, waved quickly at Alex, and then pointed at the basketball Ava held in the crook of her elbow. "So are you going to try out for the team?" she asked eagerly. "Everyone's saying you're really good."

"I don't know about that," said Ava, and her face reddened. "But I'm psyched to try out."

"She can spin it on the tip of her finger," said Alex loyally. "Show her," she commanded her sister.

Ava shot Alex a look, but she rotated her wrist, tossed the ball in the air, and then caught it at the tip of her finger. She let it spin for a few seconds. Then she caught it again.

"Wow! Awesome!" breathed Callie.

"Since football ended, it's been so weird, not having a practice to go to," said Ava. "My afternoons feel so long and empty."

Callie nodded. "Well, just so you know, during basketball season, we won't have practice right after school every day. Because gym time is in such demand, sometimes we'll be having practices at night. But you get used to it."

Ava could tell Alex's eyebrows were raised without even looking at her.

"Gotta go, bell's about to ring," said Callie, and she hurried off.

Ava turned to her twin. "What?" she asked. "Why are you giving me one of your looks?"

"*Night* practices?" said Alex. "Won't those conflict with your tutoring sessions with Luke?

Mom and Dad are not going to be happy about that."

"I'm doing just fine with school," Ava scoffed. "And puh-lease, Alex. You know that basketball practice is way more important to me than tutoring!"

She flounced away to homeroom, and Alex stared after her, shaking her head. "I have a bad feeling about this, Ave," she said quietly to her sister's retreating figure.

Alex headed in the other direction, toward her homeroom. Lindsey Davis fell into step with her. "Emily and I want to start planning this year's Christmas party," she said. "You absolutely must be part of the planning—you're so artistic and organized."

"Thanks!" said Alex. She flushed with relief. Things with Lindsey seemed completely fine. And she was glad Lindsey still wanted her help planning things, after some of their plans to celebrate Corey and Lindsey's anniversary hadn't panned out so well.

At the door of Mr. Kenerson's classroom, Lindsey put a hand on Alex's arm and leaned in. "Hey, by the way, how was your student council meeting last week?" she asked eagerly.

Alex looked at her blankly. "My student council meeting? It was fine. A little boring. We talked about fund-raising for the eighth-grade field trip. Why?"

"I just wondered if my name came up."

"*Your* name?" asked Alex. "Why would your name come up at a student government meeting?"

"Oh, no reason," said Lindsey casually. "Just wanted to see if maybe Johnny—oh my gosh, don't look. Here comes Corey."

Corey was approaching from the other direction. Alex watched a flicker of emotions race across his broad, handsome face as he saw first her and then Lindsey. Then he looked glumly down at the ground and hurried past them without saying anything.

Is Lindsey staring at me funny? Does she suspect that something's up? Alex could feel her face get warm.

"Whatever," said Lindsey, shrugging with exaggerated indifference. The bell rang for homeroom, and she headed into Mr. Kenerson's classroom.

Alex took one last glance at Corey and quickly followed Lindsey in before the bell could stop ringing.

Alex planned to talk to Emily in social studies third period, but Emily got there out of breath just as the second bell rang, and then there was no time to talk during class because they were giving oral reports. At lunch Emily and Lindsey sat together across from Alex, so she had no chance then, either. She finally caught Emily alone just after the last bell rang that afternoon.

"Em! Wait up!" called Alex, running to catch up to her friend. She slowed to a walk. Running looked too desperate.

"Hey, Alex," said Emily. "I'm staying after today. A bunch of kids are headed to the gym. Between seasons we're allowed to go to the gym and hang out, and some kids shoot baskets and stuff. You should come!"

Alex had been planning to go straight home to finalize her Christmas present shopping list, but she realized this was an important social networking opportunity. Plus, it would be an excellent chance to find out more about Corey and Lindsey. "Sounds great!" she said.

Emily smiled and hooked her arm through Alex's as they set off for the gym. Alex racked her brain for a natural way to bring up Lindsey and Corey's breakup before they joined the others, but nothing came to mind.

"So what's the deal with Lindsey and Corey?" she finally blurted out.

They'd reached the gym and were headed toward the bleachers. A bunch of cheerleaders and football players were hanging out there. Alex saw Lindsey, but, she noted with relief, Corey was not there. At the far end of the gym, Alex could see her sister playing half-court basketball with some other girls.

"I think things are okay," said Emily. "I mean, she was upset because he broke up with her before she broke up with him, but she'll get over it. And she's pretty into Johnny Morton now—remember how she was gushing about him when we were in Austin?"

"Do you think he likes her back?" Alex was impressed that Lindsey was so confidently pursuing an eighth grader. And of course—that's why she had asked about the student council meeting. Johnny was the eighth-grade class president!

"There's Lindz! She's waving to us!"

The two girls climbed up into the bleachers,

where Lindsey moved over to make room for them. Alex tried to determine whether Lindsey's smile was genuine, but she wasn't great at reading faces that carefully.

On the other side of Lindsey, Charlotte Huang and Rosa Navarro were painting each other's fingernails with a sparkly green shade. Alex wondered if Charlotte had brought the polish from New York—she'd just moved from there—and if it was the latest color.

"I'm so glad you guys are finally here!" said Lindsey. "We need to plan the Christmas party!"

"So I was thinking it should be the Saturday *after* Christmas," said Emily. "Because no one will be able to come the weekend before—everyone seems to have family stuff to do."

Lindsey clapped her hands and bounced in her seat. "We should totally do a Secret Santa gift exchange," she said. "And everyone should wear an ugly Christmas sweater—we've done that the past few years and it's been so fun!"

"Alex, will you guys be back from Massachusetts the Saturday after Christmas?" asked Emily.

Alex jumped guiltily. She'd been watching the gym doors to see if Corey had arrived.

"What? Oh! Yes, we will definitely be back by that night," she said. Was Lindsey looking at her funny?

"The only thing is, my parents won't let me host it," said Lindsey. "Because we just had that Halloween party, and my mom is still trying to get the face paint off the couch cushions."

Emily bit her lip. "There's no way can I host it," she said. "We're having thirty relatives for Christmas this year—and half of them are staying with us."

"I already asked Charlotte," said Lindsey, "but she says her parents are doing a total renovation of the kitchen."

"That's right," said Charlotte, who'd overheard. She waved her fingers in the air to dry them. "Like, a total renovation. We've been eating out at restaurants every single night." She turned back to Rosa, who was waiting to paint the next coat.

There was a pause. Alex looked anxiously from Emily to Lindsey, neither of whom was looking at her.

"Why don't *I* host it?" she suggested. As soon as the words were out of her mouth, she regretted them.

"*Would* you?" squealed Emily, grasping her arm and hugging her tightly.

"That would be amazing!" said Lindsey, and her smile seemed genuine.

"Awesome!" said Charlotte and Rosa at the same time.

Alex gulped. Her house wasn't very big. And she vaguely recalled her mom saying that their flight back from Boston was midday on Saturday. That wasn't much time to get ready for a huge party the very same night. But she'd figure it out. This was an important social undertaking for her. "Sure," she said. "My dad is a great baker, so I'll ask him to make Christmas cookies. And my mom makes this amazing turkey chili with corn bread. I used to love it, although of course I don't eat it now that I'm a vegetarian." She remembered that the last time her mother had made turkey chili, it had simmered for hours on the stove, but she put that thought out of her mind. Her mom could make it ahead, before they left for Boston, and freeze it. That would probably be even easier than making it the day of!

"Em and I will come over to help you with the decorations, of course," said Lindsey eagerly.

"Decorations?" repeated Alex weakly.

"Yes, and let's see," said Emily, pulling out her notebook. "Besides Charlotte and Rosa, we'll need . . . Annelise"—she was writing the list quickly—"Madison . . . Logan . . . Jack . . . Xander . . ."

"Don't forget the Fowlers," said Lindsey, "and Callie, and Tessa. Wow, there's a lot of people," she said with a laugh.

Alex laughed too, but it was a hollow laugh.

"Oh, and Ava of course, and Kylie," said Emily, still scribbling names. "And Owen, Andy, Johnny . . ." She looked up at Lindsey and grinned impishly. "I guess if we invite Johnny, we'll need to ask a few other eighth graders, so it won't look too obvious!"

Lindsey giggled.

Alex's stomach clenched up. This *was* a lot of kids. What would her mother say?

"What about Corey?" Emily asked. "Are you totally and completely over him, Lindz?"

Alex held her breath as Lindsey reflected. She couldn't believe Emily had just come right out and asked!

"Oh, pshhh," said Lindsey. "I am so over Corey." She looked sideways at Alex. "Don't you think we should invite him, Alex?"

Alex wondered if this was a trick to see how she would react. She nodded warily.

Lindsey's expression was unreadable. "Look, he's down there playing basketball with your sister. Maybe he has a crush on *her*! Ha-ha!"

"Ha-ha," said Alex weakly. "I somehow doubt that. They've been pals for a while, from football." She permitted herself a glance at Corey, who must have just come in. Was he looking her way? She allowed herself a tiny burst of hope. Maybe this would all work out. Especially if Lindsey really did start going out with Johnny Morton!

"I'm not sure he's totally over *you* though, Lindz," said Emily, nudging Lindsey with her elbow. "Look how he keeps looking over here. Maybe he's regretting breaking up with you!"

Lindsey looked pleased. Alex's hope dissipated.

Luckily, Emily turned the conversation back to Christmas party plans.

"Great," she said. She tore the page from her notebook and handed it to Alex. "We can talk more about this later. Alex is the perfect person to organize this party. This is going to be the best one ever."

Alex nodded. "Best one ever," she croaked.

CHAPTER THREE

"Our team is going to be the best one ever!" said Callie, as she rebounded Ava's swished shot and chest-passed it back to her. Ava stepped sideways to the corner of the key and launched another shot. It swished through the net with a satisfying *thwop*.

"With Ava able to shoot from outside, that will keep zones from collapsing and give us forwards some breathing room!" said Madison Jackson. She rebounded a basket Ava missed and laid it back in. "We had no good outside shooting last year."

Ava grinned. It felt so nice to be playing sports again. And it was such a relief that there was a girls' basketball team. She wouldn't have to be the center of any media firestorms, the way she'd been on the football team as the only girl. She was not a fan of lots of attention. Unlike her twin sister. She glanced across the gym to where Alex sat, chatting away with a big group of popular seventh graders. She was happy to see Alex was sitting next to Lindsey. Maybe there wouldn't be drama about Corey after all. Where *was* Corey, anyway? She was surprised not to see him here on an open-gym day.

"Hey! You guys want to go threes?"

There he was. Corey had walked over, cradling a basketball under his arm. Next to him were Jack Valdeavano and Xander Browning. Ava felt her face get a little warm. She still kind of, sort of liked Jack, even though the one time they'd tried to go on a date had been really disastrous. They'd decided to go back to just being friends, but she couldn't help it if she blushed every time she saw him. She was glad she was probably already flushed from exertion.

"You got it," said Callie. "Girls against boys."

The game was close. Ava guarded Jack. She knew his game well by this point, having played with him many times at the little park near their house. She knew he was a lefty with a quick first step and that he liked to drive baseline. He, however, knew she had a quick release, and he guarded her outside shot closely. The boys won in a tiebreaker.

They all stood, panting. Ava felt good about the way she'd played. She made a note to herself to work on her left-hand layup over the holiday break.

"Ava, you should come to the rec center tonight," said Callie. "A bunch of us are going there around eight to scrimmage."

Ava started to say yes, and then remembered that Luke Grabowski, her tutor, was supposed to come over for a session tonight.

"Uh, can I give you a definite maybe?" said Ava. "I need to rearrange some stuff, but I'm pretty sure I can get there." She pictured what her mother's face would look like when she asked her. Mrs. Sackett would probably not see eye to eye with her about the need to cancel her session with Luke, but Ava figured she might as well start the conversation now, and explain to her parents that she no longer needed Luke's help, especially as she'd be having night practices once the season started. There *was* the nagging issue of the persuasive essay that was due next Monday. Mr. Rader had suggested she get started on it tonight. But that wasn't necessary—she had all week to write it.

"Play again?" said Jack. He flicked the ball underhand to Corey at the top of the key.

The ball whacked Corey in the shoulder and dribbled away.

Corey started guiltily and trotted after the ball. Ava groaned inwardly. He hadn't been watching for the pass because he'd been staring across the gym with a moony expression on his face.

At Alex.

Ava and Alex took the late bus home. Ava let Alex natter away about Corey, and the Christmas party, and Lindsey's crush on Johnny Morton, the eighth-grade class president. Ava nodded and murmured from time to time, but she was thinking about basketball, and how to break it to her parents that she no longer needed Luke's help. They'd understand. They had to.

"Lindsey and Emily said it's a tradition to make it an ugly sweater theme party," said Alex with a frown. "After all the cute holiday outfits I assembled! Oh well. Of course I don't own any ugly sweaters, but they said we can all go to the thrift store to shop for them—evidently shopping for ugly sweaters is another annual tradition. You should totally come with us, Ave."

"What? Sure," said Ava. She barely registered what Alex was saying—she was trying to decide if it'd be better to talk to her parents at dinner, with Alex and Tommy there, or after dinner. Alex hadn't been particularly supportive of her basketball tryout, but she knew Tommy would be. She decided to do it at dinner.

But soon it was halfway through their meal, and Ava couldn't even begin to bring up the subject of the rec center scrimmage, because Alex kept talking on and on about the upcoming Christmas party, and the theme of ugly sweaters, and the Secret Santa gift exchange.

Mom seems distracted, Ava thought. *And Coach does too,* she realized. They seemed happy to let Alex talk and talk and talk.

Tommy finally got Alex's attention by balling up his napkin and throwing it at her.

". . . and it's a tradition to go to the thrift store and—hey!" She stopped midsentence.

"Al, this is fascinating and all, but you're

making my head hurt, talking Christmas this early in December," he said. He turned to Ava. "So how's the team look?" he asked.

Ava shot him a grateful look. "I think we're going to be pretty good," she said. "And as a matter of fact, some of the girls invited me to go to the rec center tonight, to scrimmage with them. Can I go, Mom?"

"What, honey?" Her mom looked up, as though Ava had startled her out of her thoughts. "Oh, sure," she said distractedly.

"Thanks!" said Ava. She'd been worried for no reason! Of course her parents would be understanding about basketball taking priority over Luke and tutoring.

"Just as long as it's not tonight. Because Luke is coming over at seven."

Ava choked on her sip of milk. "But Mom, see, that's the thing. I don't think I need Luke anymore," she said hurriedly. "I'm doing great—well, just fine—in all—well, in most of—my classes. And once real practices start, I'm going to have to see Luke less anyway, because we'll be practicing in the evenings a lot and—"

"Michael," said Mrs. Sackett, in an all-business tone.

Coach started coughing.

Mrs. Sackett glared at him. "Ava," she said. "About basketball. We need to have a discussion."

The table suddenly went quiet.

"Al? Tom? How about you guys go start your homework?" suggested Coach.

Alex and Tommy got the hint. They slid out of their chairs and bolted for the hallway. Ava heard them both stomping up the stairs.

She looked from her mother to her father. Neither seemed to want to be the first to speak.

"What?" asked Ava. "Why are you guys looking at me like that? Okay, okay, I guess it's short notice to cancel on Luke now. I don't *have* to go to the rec center tonight. . . ." Her voice trailed off.

"Ava," said her mother. "Your father and I have been talking. And we think—at least, I think, and your father agrees—that it would be good for you to take a season off from sports to concentrate on your studying."

Coach was suddenly extremely interested in a spot on the table.

"Oh, wait. Is this about the bad grade I got on the math test last week?" asked Ava. "Because that was a total fluke. I just forgot to bring home the study guide the night before, and Mrs. Vargas—"

Mrs. Sackett frowned.

"Is it that dumb lab report I turned in one day late? That will so not happen again—see, I left that on the floor of the car and—" Ava stopped. Her parents exchanged another look. She seemed to be digging herself deeper into a hole. Maybe they didn't even *know* about these incidents. "Coach!" she said, giving her father a beseeching look. "You don't agree with this, do you?"

Coach cleared his throat. "Well, Ava, I actually—yes, I do. We've gotten a few e-mails from some of your teachers. They're concerned that you've let your grades slide recently."

"But maybe that's because I'm *between* sports right now!" Ava jumped in. "My grades were better when I had the structure of practice and games! Don't you see?"

Mrs. Sackett put a hand on Ava's arm. "Honey, I've been looking into the basketball team for a while, and when I found out they sometimes hold evening practices I asked Mrs. Hyde if she didn't think this change in your study schedule could be a problem. We've tried hard to help you be consistent with your study habits, and with basketball and nighttime practices, the whole routine will be disrupted. She agreed that the nighttime practices would pose a challenge. Your father and I have been meaning to discuss this with you."

Ava stared from her mother to her father, horror written across her face. She stood up from the table and left the house without a word, letting the door slam behind her.

CHAPTER FOUR

Ava stomped across the driveway to where she'd left her basketball near the garage. She muttered to herself, imagining angry words she should have said to her parents.

She picked up the ball and launched it at the basket. Air ball.

At the end of football season, Coach had finally, finally, finally put up a basketball hoop in the driveway. She'd been begging him to do it since they'd moved there in July.

But right now she was so mad she couldn't aim straight. Most of her shots clanged off the backboard.

"Wow," said a voice in the growing darkness.

"Ease up there, Ave." It was Luke Grabowski, her tutor. He was one of Tommy's friends, and normally Ava liked seeing him.

The ball bounced his way. He scooped it up, set down his backpack, and took a shot. It banked in neatly.

For some reason this just made Ava madder.

"Hey," said Luke, letting the ball roll away, where it came to rest alongside the fence. "What's up? You're not your usual chipper self."

Ava started to tell him about basketball, but stopped. She didn't want to hurt his feelings. After all, her sessions with him were a big part of the reason her parents weren't letting her play. "I'm fine," she said dully. "Come on inside. You can help me figure out how to conjugate irregular verbs in Spanish."

She turned and stomped up the steps.

Alex knocked gently on Ava's door later that night, after Luke had left. She heard a muffled "Go away" from inside, but she pushed open the door anyway.

Her sister was lying in her bed, under the

covers, still fully dressed. She had her Spanish textbook propped open on her knees, but Alex felt certain she hadn't been looking at it.

"Hey," said Alex, moving into the room to sit down on Ava's bed.

"Hey," replied Ava.

"I think I found the perfect outfit to wear on the plane to Boston," said Alex, trying to sound cheerful.

Ava didn't look up. She grunted and turned a page.

"And it's going to be so fun, having the party here. I'm still getting used to the idea of the ugly sweater theme, but I guess if everyone is wearing one—" She broke off. Ava didn't seem to be interested in talking about the party. "Hey, I'm really sorry about basketball," Alex said softly.

Ava finally looked up at her. "It's so not fair," she said. "I'm being penalized because I have ADHD."

"I think Mom and Dad mean well," said Alex, who of course had been eavesdropping on the conversation in the kitchen from a listening post at the top of the stairs.

Ava's green eyes flashed.

"And you know, maybe they have a point,

about giving you structure and consistency with your study habits," said Alex. As soon as the words were out of her mouth, she regretted them.

Ava shot her a reproachful look. "Thanks for the support," she said bitterly.

Alex gulped. "Sorry, Ava, I didn't mean—"

Ava dumped her textbook onto the floor.

The sound made Alex jump. "Well, see you in the morning," she said quickly, and bolted from the room.

Ava was late getting downstairs for breakfast the next morning—which was nothing new. To make amends, Alex toasted a bagel for her and was just slathering it with peanut butter when Ava appeared in the kitchen with her backpack on and her wet hair showing comb marks.

Coach and Tommy had already left for school. Mrs. Sackett was upstairs getting dressed.

"Thanks," Ava said gruffly as Alex handed her the bagel on the paper towel. "Let's get going so I don't have to pretend to be cheerful."

When they got to school, Ava quickly shoved

her stuff into her overflowing locker and muttered good-bye to Alex.

Alex was still frowning after her sister when she heard a low voice speak in her ear.

"Hey. Quick question for you."

Alex felt her knees buckle slightly when she turned around and saw that it was Corey. But she managed not to choke on the words as she said, "Sure! What's up?"

"Number three on the math homework? Did you get a negative answer?"

Alex's mind raced. Should she pretend to think it over, or just tell him yes right away? Because of course she had total recall of her homework answers. There had only been seven math problems. "Yes, I had a negative number," she said, choosing the latter option.

"Cool," he said, and grinned. He had such a nice smile.

"Hey, guys!"

Alex's breath caught in her throat. Lindsey!

She felt Corey tense up next to her. She instinctively moved a few inches away from him.

If Lindsey was bothered by their being together, she didn't say anything. "Just to let you know, we're choosing Secret Santas at lunch today," she said. "Spread the word!" She turned and hurried away.

"Okay!" said Alex and Corey at the exact same time.

Corey muttered a quick good-bye and hurried off.

At lunch, everyone wrote their names on scraps of paper and put them into Corey's baseball cap. Kids weren't allowed to wear hats during the school day, but Emily had asked him to bring it to lunch. They passed the hat around and everyone drew a name.

Alex watched Ava unfold her paper, read the name, and blush. *Ha! She must have chosen Jack,* Alex thought. When it was Alex's turn to choose, she found to her dismay that she'd selected Rosa. Of all the people whose names were in the hat, Rosa's was the one she'd have least wanted to select. It wasn't like they didn't like each other, exactly. They just didn't seem to click the way Alex did with most of the others. Plus, she had no idea what Rosa's interests were, outside of cheerleading.

Charlotte picked next. She peeked at the name and smiled. "Ha!" she said. "I know just the thing for my Secret Sant-ee. We're going to New York City for Christmas, of course, and there's this ultracool boutique in Tribeca that just opened where you simply can't go wrong."

Alex saw several dismayed faces around the table. She was kind of happy that Charlotte had recently joined her group of friends, because it meant she and Ava weren't the new kids anymore. And Charlotte was even more clueless than Alex was sometimes. Charlotte's family had an enormous house, and Alex was pretty sure they even had servants, but not everyone else did. She quickly thought of a way to even the playing field in terms of gifts.

"Hey! I have an idea!" she said brightly. "Why don't we all *make* our presents this year?"

"Great idea!" said Emily, almost too quickly.

Lots of other kids nodded.

Charlotte wrinkled her brow. "*Make* them? You mean, like pot holders and stuff?"

Alex laughed. "There are lots of things you can make," she said. "I'm sure you'll think of something great."

"And homemade presents will fit in perfectly

with the ugly sweater theme," added Emily.

"About that," said Charlotte. "I have no clue where to shop for an ugly sweater."

Alex quickly explained to her about the planned thrift store outing, and invited her along.

Corey grinned. "The sight of you in a thrift store will be something to see," he said to Charlotte.

Charlotte didn't seem offended by Corey's remark. *That's the thing about Corey,* Alex thought. *He knows how to tease without ever coming across as mean.* She stopped herself from smiling at him across the table.

"And with Alex there to guide us to make the right fashion choices, we'll be ready for the runway," continued Corey with an earnest grin in her direction.

Alex had to pretend to drop her napkin and hide under the table, so people wouldn't see how much she was blushing.

CHAPTER FIVE

"Ava, I noticed you didn't pass in a thesis statement for your persuasive essay yesterday," said Mr. Rader. He'd asked Ava to stop by to see him before leaving for her next class.

Ava stared down at her sneakers. The white rubber toes were covered in flowers that her friend Kylie had drawn. "Yeah, I know," she said. "I'm still thinking about what to write. I'm trying to decide between, um, why we should have a later start time to our school day and why we should have a longer lunch hour." In fact, she hadn't thought much about her topic at all, but those topics were as good as any. She couldn't imagine writing four pages' worth of stuff on any topic.

Mr. Rader lowered his chin and frowned at her over the tops of his glasses. "Well, decide soon, Ava. As you know, the outline is due Thursday. I may need to have a word with Mrs. Hyde about helping you narrow down your arguments and supporting a thesis statement," he said.

Ava shook her head. "I'm on it, Mr. Rader, I promise," she said.

He nodded. "Run along or you'll be late for your next class," he said.

Ava's heart sank as she swung her backpack onto her shoulder and headed out. If Mr. Rader spoke to Mrs. Hyde, her parents were sure to find out. She thought about the Spanish test she'd taken this morning. She had to admit, it was a good thing Luke had been there last night to drill her on her irregular verbs, because she would have bombed it otherwise. Still. Couldn't her parents see that she was doing worse, not better, without sports? This winter could be a disaster both athletically *and* academically.

A thought struck her. She'd try appealing directly to her father. He was a *coach*, and he'd once been an athlete. He would listen to reason.

"Ava!" called Madison. "Are you coming to the gym after school today to play?"

The final bell had just rung, and Ava couldn't get out of the middle school fast enough.

"Can't today," said Ava.

"You didn't come to the rec center last night!" Madison reproached her. "You're not having second thoughts about coming out for the team, are you?"

"Me? No," said Ava quickly. "*I* am definitely not having second thoughts."

She left it at that. There was no need to go public with her parents' ridiculous decree just yet. She felt sure she could get through to Coach.

Ashland High was just across the parking lot from the middle school. The high schoolers had gotten out earlier, but Ava knew where to find her father. He oversaw the weight-training kids—mostly fall and spring athletes who didn't do a formal winter sport.

She could hear the clanking of weights and

blasting of music before she'd even turned the corner of the hallway that led to the weight room. Inside it was hot and crowded with high school kids, many of whom she recognized from the football team. She saw Tommy standing behind his friend Winston on the bench press, but knew better than to distract him while he was spotting.

Coach noticed her almost immediately. He waved and beckoned her over to where he was scribbling some notes on a clipboard.

"Ave!" He shouted to be heard over the clanging weights. "What brings you here?"

She pointed toward the doorway, indicating that she wanted to talk in quieter surroundings, and he nodded and strode after her.

Once in the hallway, she turned and looked at him with a pleading expression. "Coach," she began. "About me not playing basketball. I was hoping to talk it over with you calmly and rationally."

Coach stiffened. He pressed his lips together and nodded guardedly.

"See, I have a feeling this is not your decision and that it's coming mostly from Mom," said Ava. "Because you know sports so well, and you know that—"

He held up a hand to stop her.

"Ava, I realize it's a disappointment to you," he said. "But it was a decision your mother and I made together. I can't have you blaming your mother for what we concluded was the best thing for you right now. We're trying to help you impose structure on your life, so you can be successful academically. Academics always come before sports, and you know how firmly I believe that. And that's that. Now, I really have to get back inside to oversee." And with a quick pat on her shoulder, he left her standing there, grinding her teeth in frustration.

Ava walked home from school so she could practice her dribbling, even though her hopes of changing her parents' minds were fading as fast as the fall afternoon light. She didn't cry. To cry would be to admit that her parents had won, and she wasn't yet ready to accept their decision as final.

As she passed the park on Saragaso Way, she spotted Jack shooting around. She stopped dribbling and held her ball tightly with both hands, watching him work on a reverse layup. Why hadn't he just stayed at school to play with the rest of the kids at the gym? She felt a slight shock zing down her spine. Was it because she hadn't been there? Was he hoping *she* would walk past this park?

She knew that Alex had guessed she'd picked Jack when they drew names for Secret Santa, because Alex and Ava could usually read what was going through each other's minds in situations like that. She hoped she hadn't turned red or something. For now, what she and Jack had was just a friendship. Still, she needed to figure out what on earth she was going to make for him for a Secret Santa present. Good at crafts she was not, and it was supposed to be something homemade.

"Hey!" she called to him. She scrambled down the grassy incline and cut a diagonal through the park.

In answer, he passed the ball to her and pointed toward the rim to indicate that she should shoot from where she was. She dropped all her stuff and took a long-range jumper. It almost went in.

Jack grinned and retrieved the ball. Then he

passed it back to her. "I was hoping you'd come along," he said.

"Why? So I could school you in one-on-one?" she teased.

"Um, sure. Yeah, that, plus I need you to help me figure out what that sister of yours would want for a Secret Santa present."

"Don't tell me you got Alex," said Ava.

"Okay, I won't," he said.

"You got *Alex*?"

"No. But I know the person who did, and that person wants me to ask you for tips because that person knows I know you."

"You're making my head hurt," said Ava. "But I will think about it and get back to you."

"Thanks," he said. "So, you want to play?"

She sighed. "I can't. I have to go work on my dumb thesis statement for my dumb persuasive essay, which is way overdue. But as long as we're asking each other cryptic questions—I happen to know the person who is your Secret Santa, and that person asked me to ask you what you want."

Jack grinned. "Food," he said. "You can't go wrong with food. I'm always hungry."

Ava laughed. "Okay, I'll tell the person to

get you a few bags of frozen lima beans and a bushel of brussels sprouts."

"Awesome," he said. He waved good-bye and went back to shooting baskets.

When Ava got home, she smelled vegetable lasagna baking. Her mother was on the phone in the kitchen. Mrs. Sackett waved to Ava, and then moved through the swinging door into the hallway, still talking to the other person in a low voice. Ava couldn't make out the words, but she got the distinct impression that her mother did not want her to listen in.

Alex, who'd come home on the late bus, walked in just a minute after Ava did. "It was so fun hanging out at the gym," she said to Ava, who was searching through the fruit bowl for the perfect apple. "But I didn't get any further with the Corey-Lindsey situation. I'm just not able to tell whether Lindsey cares if Corey and I start liking each other."

Ava took a bite of the apple she'd grabbed with one hand and then opened the oven door with the other. She peered in at the lasagna, which was starting to bubble and brown. It smelled amazing. She closed it and turned to face Alex. "Honestly, Al, I don't think it's really fair for Lindsey to be upset," she said. "I mean, they've broken up. It's not like Corey is supposed to be in mourning for the rest of his middle school career or anything."

"I know, but I just don't want to risk losing Lindsey as a friend."

Ava sighed in exasperation. This whole situation made her head hurt. She didn't understand why everything had to be so complicated. She decided to change the subject. "Have you noticed that Mom has been really secretive recently?" she asked. "I mean, just a minute ago when I walked in, she was on the phone, and she immediately left the room so I wouldn't hear her conversation."

"Hmm," said Alex. "That *is* strange. I wonder if it's a Christmas surprise. Maybe she's arranging some big event with our old friends back home?"

Just then their mother came back into the kitchen, smiling pleasantly, and, Ava thought, a little artificially. Ava was still upset with her mom, but she knew better than to act sulky. She was still holding out hope that she could change her mother's mind about basketball.

"Girls, I have a favor to ask you," she said as

she put the phone back in its cradle. "You know my friend Mrs. Barnaby, who runs the day-care center at the community college? They're having their staff holiday party on Thursday afternoon and need coverage for the kids for just a couple of hours. I told her you girls could help out. Ava, you'll have plenty of time to get your homework done, as you'll be home before dinner."

"Oh, is *that* who you were just talking to?" asked Alex. "We thought you were involved in some sort of high-level, top-secret negotiation!"

Mrs. Sackett furrowed her brow. "Just now? Oh! No, that wasn't Mrs. Barnaby just now. That was—" She seemed to reconsider what she'd been about to say. "That was someone else."

Ava and Alex exchanged a look.

Something is definitely going on, Ava thought.

CHAPTER SIX

On Wednesday after school a big group of Ashland Middle schoolers met up outside the school and walked to Carolee's Consignment store in search of ugly Christmas sweaters. Emily had called ahead to let Carolee know that they were coming.

"She says she looks forward to this every Christmas," said Emily, as the group approached the store. "All year long, she collects and sets aside a huge bunch of sweaters just for us!"

"I've never been to a thrift store," Charlotte admitted.

"I'm pretty sure none of the boys have either," said Emily.

"Now that's just not true," said Corey, pretending to sound offended. "Jack and I come here at least once a week, don't we, Jack?"

"Oh, sure, O'Sullivan, sure," said Jack with exaggerated enthusiasm. "How else do you think I always find that 'perfect accessory'?" He crooked his fingers into air quotes.

Alex laughed. This was such a fun, rare opportunity to hang out outside of school with their guy friends! Even Ava seemed excited about it, and Alex couldn't remember the last time Ava had looked enthusiastic about shopping.

She stole a glance at Lindsey. Was she upset that Johnny Morton wasn't with them? He'd had a dentist appointment or something. Alex wondered if Lindsey was intentionally walking near Corey and Jack, or if that was just a coincidence of walking in a big clump. She couldn't stop analyzing every little thing that Lindsey did.

Carolee greeted them warmly as they filed in. Although she was an older woman, Alex liked her style: upswept reddish hair, lots of necklaces, a plain but well-tailored black dress.

"There's a whole collection of Christmas cheer on that circular rack over there," she said. "Have fun!"

Alex found the perfect sweater almost immediately. It was bright pink with green accents and big white snowflakes on the front. And the best thing was there were actual twinkling lights at the end of each snowflake. A tiny wire was stitched into the side seam and was attached to a small on-off switch that you could keep in your pocket. The lights didn't work, but Alex wondered if her mother could replace the bulbs or something. "Please let this fit!" she whispered, heading for the dressing room.

The changing rooms were small, with even smaller mirrors. Alex could barely turn around to see what her sweater looked like from the back. She'd seen a large, three-way mirror in the corridor of the changing area, so she stepped out to have a look—

—and almost collided with Corey, who was coming out of the changing room across the corridor.

He was wearing a ridiculously bright purple sweater vest with two big snowmen on the front. The garish color clashed hideously with his usually gorgeous red hair.

Alex forgot to be nervous. She guffawed with laughter at the sight of him.

He grinned. "Guess that's the response I'm going for," he said. "You look pretty awesome yourself. Do those lights work?"

Alex turned to survey herself in the mirror. Of course it was an ugly sweater, but the bright-green trim actually complemented her green eyes, and the overall effect was, well, kind of snappy. Plus, she'd found a sparkly green hair clip that almost perfectly matched her sweater—and it looked really nice in her hair. It wasn't ugly, either. It was versatile enough to look good with anything. She wasn't planning to actually buy it, but she always tried to accessorize when she tried something on, just to see the potential. Her mother had told her she had good instincts when it came to fashion.

The sweater was a little big for her, but that just made it look even funnier. "The lights don't work, but I'm going to try to get them fixed," she said. "What do you think? How do I look?"

Corey flushed so much that his cheeks matched her pink sweater. "It would be hard for you not to look awesome," he said in a quiet voice.

Alex felt an electric thrill zoom up and down her entire body. She didn't dare say anything, which was probably a good thing because at that moment, Lindsey swung open the door of her own changing room and stood right between them. They both jumped back a step as though they'd been stung.

"Great sweaters," said Lindsey, smiling sweetly at them. She was holding a small armful of sweaters.

"Thanks," said Alex and Corey at the same moment.

"I love that hair clip, Alex," said Lindsey. "It almost looks like it came with the sweater!"

"Ha-ha!" said Alex. She whipped it out of her hair. "I don't have enough money for the sweater *and* the hair thing, but I just figured I'd try it on." She and Corey each ducked inside their changing rooms.

Alex leaned against the wall, gathering her wits. This was all so confusing!

Most of her friends managed to find a sweater they liked—or thought was appropriately ugly. Ava's was huge and baggy—almost like a sweaterdress. Kylie found a sweater with a cowboy Santa. Logan's was a pretty ordinary Christmas sweater, but it was clearly meant for a girl, which made it look really funny on him.

Charlotte took the longest to pick one. In the end she bought several sweaters so she'd be able to decide the day of the party.

Mrs. Sackett came to pick up Ava and Alex, as well as Emily, Lindsey, and Charlotte, all of whom lived along the route home.

"Did you find your sweaters?" asked Mrs. Sackett as they pulled away.

"Did I!" squealed Charlotte. "I couldn't decide among four different sweaters, so I bought them all!"

"This is going to be the best party ever," said Emily.

"Thanks so much for agreeing to host it, Mrs. Sackett," added Lindsey.

Mrs. Sackett suddenly coughed, but managed to recover her breath.

"Oh, and Mrs. Sackett, my mom said to tell you that she knows an awesome caterer," added Charlotte. "He makes *the* best passed hors d'oeuvres."

Alex, who was sitting in the front passenger seat, saw the smile evaporate from her mother's face. Luckily, the other girls were busy chatting away in the back and didn't appear to notice.

A thought occurred to Alex. Had she forgotten

to mention to her mother that the Sacketts were going to be hosting the party? Surely not. She was 90 percent, well, maybe 78 percent sure she'd mentioned that detail at dinner the night she told her parents about the party. Maybe 60 percent . . .

As soon as they'd deposited Charlotte at her house, and it was just Alex, Ava, and Mrs. Sackett, their mother cleared her throat.

"So. I understand you said we would host the party, Alex?" she asked.

Alex swallowed hard. "Right. About that. Didn't I mention it?"

"No, as a matter of fact, you didn't."

"I thought I had."

"You hadn't."

"Oops, ha-ha," said Alex. In the backseat, directly behind Alex, Ava was being zero help. She was probably staring morosely out the window, lost in thought. Alex didn't dare turn and look at her.

"I know it's the day we get back from Boston," Alex said. Her words tumbled out quickly so her mother couldn't interrupt. "But, see, I was thinking we could do all the cooking before we leave—I'll help a ton, of course—and you could make your famous turkey chili and—"

"Alex."

"—and Daddy could bake some Christmas cookies, and of course I'd help with those, too, because I know the decorating can be pretty time-consuming, and—"

"Alex!"

"—and it's a great group of kids, not too many, well, at least not *that* many, and—"

"Alexandra!"

Her mother's voice was sharp. Alex stopped talking.

They were pulling into their driveway. Mrs. Sackett parked and turned off the engine. Then she turned to face Alex.

"Alex, we cannot host this Christmas party," she said.

"But I already told—"

Mrs. Sackett held up a hand to silence her. "We don't have the money to spend on throwing a party for your friends right now," she said. "What with the holidays, and the expenses I'm incurring with this big pottery order, and—well, and lots of other things, we just can't manage it right now. You ought to have asked me, and you didn't. I'm sorry you're now in this predicament, but you have only yourself to blame."

Alex thought her mother sounded more upset than mad. That was weird.

Mrs. Sackett's phone rang, and she frowned at the caller's number. She answered without even saying hello. "One second, I can't talk right now," she said with a quick glance back at the girls. She collected her purse and exited the car before she resumed the conversation.

"Awesome," said Ava dully.

"This is an unmitigated disaster," said Alex.

"I thought you'd asked Mom's permission, Alex. How could you have neglected to mention the little detail that we were having the party at our house?"

Alex sighed heavily. "I thought I *had* mentioned it."

"Mom sounded upset," observed Ava. "Like there's something bigger going on and she doesn't want to tell us. Did you notice how she just answered that call? Like it's some mysterious person she doesn't want us to know about?"

"Maybe it's a loan shark," said Alex worriedly.

"A what shark?"

"You know, one of those mean guys who lends you money and then kills you if you don't pay them back."

"I highly doubt that," Ava scoffed. "But do you think they're having money troubles?"

"How could they? Daddy's job can't be in trouble. He won State!"

Ava shrugged. "Something definitely seems to be up."

Alex was too immersed in her own problems to hazard any guesses. Her mind was working overtime.

"So what are you going to say to everyone?"

Alex furrowed her brow. This called for some strategic planning, and strategic planning was one of her strengths. "I won't say anything," she said simply.

Ava gave her a confused look.

"I'll just have to get Mom to change her mind."

"Yeah, good luck with that," said Ava gloomily. "Let's hope you have more success than I'm having convincing her to let me play basketball."

CHAPTER SEVEN

Thursday afternoon, Ava followed Alex into the community college day-care center to report for duty. Considering how concerned her parents seemed to be about Ava's study habits, Ava thought it was odd that her mom should so readily volunteer her to work at the day-care center for the afternoon. On the other hand, Ava had to admit, it was only for two hours. And she liked little kids.

"Did you get your outline in today?" asked Alex.

"Yep," said Ava glumly. "Now I get to try to come up with at least three ideas why we should have a longer lunch hour. It all seems so pointless."

Alex frowned. "Maybe you should have picked a more interesting topic."

Ava shrugged. "It's schoolwork. It's *supposed* to be uninteresting," she said.

Alex gave her a pained look as they headed inside.

"Thank you girls, so very much," said Mrs. Barnaby in a quiet voice that was just above a whisper. "Most of them are napping now, and then it will be snack time, so I don't think they'll be too high energy for you," she said. "Just as long as Dougie stays asleep," she added, more to herself than to the girls.

"No problem, Mrs. Barnaby," said Alex. "We're happy to help out."

She gave them instructions for snack time and showed them quickly around the different areas of the large, cheerful room.

Ava eyed the changing table. "I thought they were all potty trained," she said.

"Oh, most of them are," said Mrs. Barnaby, laughing lightly. "And those who aren't will let you know!"

Ava swallowed. Maybe this wouldn't be as much of a breeze as she'd hoped.

"And we'll be just down the hall in the college

cafeteria if you need us," said Mrs. Barnaby.

As soon as Mrs. Barnaby had left to join the other caregivers, Ava and Alex tiptoed over to the nap room, which was darkened and quiet. The shades had been drawn, and ten small children lay on cots, sleeping contentedly.

"This shouldn't be too bad," whispered Alex. "In fact, they may nap the entire time."

"There's an empty cot over in the corner," Ava whispered back. "I wonder if—"

A sudden blast of a toy bugle near her left elbow caused her to jump a full six inches into the air. She whirled around. A tiny boy with sleep-tousled hair and a devilish grin emitted a peal of gleeful laughter, and then blasted the bugle again.

"Shh! You'll wake everyone up!" hissed Alex frantically. She lunged for the bugle, but the boy sidestepped her with surprising balance. He blasted his horn again.

Ava looked back at the nap room inhabitants and groaned. "I'm guessing that's Dougie," she said. "They're all awake now."

Someone tugged on her T-shirt. She looked down. A little girl in pigtails gazed up at Ava with big brown eyes, and then pointed at her diaper. "Change?" she said.

Another tug from her other side. A little boy stared up at her and pointed to his diaper too.

Ava groaned. "This is going to be a long two hours, Al," she said, but if Alex replied, Ava couldn't hear her over the sound of the blasting bugle.

Two hours later, their father picked them up. Ava staggered into the car, exhausted. She'd changed three diapers, had a full cup of juice spilled in her lap, and had picked up about a million wooden blocks. Alex looked a little the worse for wear too.

"How did it go, girls?" asked Coach, as they headed for home.

"Awesome," said Alex, who was trying to get orange finger paint out of her hair with a tissue.

"Remind me never to have children," added Ava.

Their dad grinned. "Well, it was nice of you to help out," he said.

"I am so ready for Christmas break," said Alex with a little groan. "And for seeing all our old friends in Massachusetts," she added.

Ava nodded. She had been thinking about some of the people she was really looking forward to seeing again. Like her old teammate and sort-of ex-boyfriend, Charlie Weidner. And a bunch of the kids from her sports teams, kids she'd grown up with and had known as long as she could remember.

She heard her sister gasp and shook herself out of her reverie. "What?" she demanded. "What's the matter, Al?"

Alex seemed too shocked to be able to respond.

"What did you just say, Coach?" asked Ava. "I missed it."

Her father took a deep breath. "I just said that I'm sorry to say, we aren't going to be going back to Massachusetts after all. At least not right now, not for Christmas," he said. His jaw twitched, as though he were bracing himself for Ava's outrage.

Which was not long in coming.

"What?" she nearly shouted. "I thought we had our tickets! You can't be serious!"

By now they were back home in their driveway. "Girls," said Coach. He turned off the engine and swiveled around to look at them. "Your mother and I discussed this, and we decided to postpone the trip. Now please help me carry in the groceries."

"But *why*?" wailed Alex, as the two girls followed their father up the driveway, laden down with shopping bags. "It's so not fair! I thought—"

Their father stepped to the side and held the door open so that the girls could go in ahead of him. Then he followed them inside. "We can talk about it later," he said, plunking his bags down on the table. "For now, I need to put away groceries, and then I have some things I need to work on in the shed. Your mother will be home soon. You girls can go start your homework."

And that seemed to be the end of the conversation.

Up in her room, Ava tried, without much success, to get started on her essay. Her mind kept wandering. She heard a lot of banging and clanging outside and went to the window. Coach was carrying tools and workbenches out of the shed and piling them on the lawn. Why on earth was he cleaning out the shed when they had just moved all their stuff into it? He probably wouldn't tell her. Both her parents were being so weird and secretive. She shrugged and flopped back down on her bed to try again with her essay.

Dinner was a gloomy, quiet affair. Obviously Tommy had heard the news about their trip, because he barely spoke. Mr. and Mrs. Sackett did most of the talking—to each other—and if they noticed that all three of their children were giving them the cold shoulder, they pretended not to.

When they finished the dishes, the three Sackett kids convened in Tommy's room.

He paced back and forth and clutched his hair with both hands. "I had this meeting lined up," he said. "With this guy from the music industry that Jaden's dad knows. We had it all planned. I was going to come to their holiday party, and he was going to introduce me, and I was going to hand the guy Trio Grande's demo and—!" He trailed off but continued to walk around the room.

"Yeah, our parents aren't exactly winning parents-of-the-year awards," said Alex bitterly. "Saying no to my party, for one."

"And not letting me play basketball," said Ava.

"And now Boston," finished Tommy. "What is *up* with them?"

No one answered. The two girls sat side by side on Tommy's bed and watched him pace. Finally Alex stood up.

"Well, I don't know about you two, but *I* see these challenges as merely a jumping-off point for us to start negotiations," said Alex.

Ava and Tommy exchanged a look. "What is she talking about?" Tommy asked Ava.

Ava shrugged.

"I'm trying to look on the positive side of the situation," said Alex. "It sounds like there's not much we can do about not going to Massachusetts."

Tommy groaned.

"But maybe now that they've told us we can't go, they'll feel so guilty about disappointing us that I should be able to talk them into having my party!" she said brightly.

"How nice for you," said Ava. Sometimes Alex could be so self-involved.

"And Ava, maybe you could even discuss their basketball decision and get them to change their minds," said Alex. "I mean, after I've talked them into letting me have the party," she added hastily. "We don't want to make too many demands at the same time."

Ava sighed. "They've got Mrs. Hyde in their corner, telling them sports are bad for kids with ADHD," she said. "No amount of convincing from me is going to talk them out of an expert's opinion."

"Well, Tommy, I'm sure we can figure out a way to make staying here in Texas over the holiday okay," said Alex.

"No, we can't," he said flatly. "That was my career you just heard getting flushed down the toilet."

"What about Cassie? You'll be able to spend some quality time with her at least."

"She's going to Kansas with her family, to visit relatives," said Tommy.

That finally seemed to dampen Alex's positive attitude. She sat back down on the bed next to Ava and put her chin in her hands. "And now we won't even get to see any snow this winter. Yeah, they definitely are not winning parents of the year," she repeated.

CHAPTER EIGHT

Friday morning Lindsey caught up with Alex before they walked into Mr. Kenerson's homeroom.

"Alex," she said gravely. "Can I talk to you privately?"

"Um, sure," said Alex, her voice high and tight. Her stomach did a cartwheel. This was it. Lindsey was going to let her have it for pouncing on her ex-boyfriend the second they'd broken up. She was going to tell Alex it was the end of their friendship. Alex would be shunned by the group. She might as well drop out of school now and ask her mom to homeschool her, or send her away somewhere. Maybe military school. Anything would be better than—

"Alex?"

Alex jumped. "Sorry," she said. "What did you want to talk to me about?"

"I wanted to make sure," said Lindsey, "that it's really okay for you guys to host the party. Your mom didn't seem too psyched about it in the car the other day, when we brought it up."

Relief eddied through Alex's entire body, like warm waves foaming around a rocky shore. It was about the party, not Corey! "Oh! That!" She laughed lightly. "Of course it's okay! My mom was just, ah, just concerned about how much turkey chili to make, that's all. We are totally psyched to have the party." She would just have to convince her parents to change their minds. Maybe if she could get them to see that not hosting this party would mean the end of Alex's social existence for the remainder of her life in Ashland, they'd understand how important it was.

Lindsey looked relieved. She smiled, her bright-white teeth glinting. "Oh, good. Well, just wanted to make sure." She gave Alex a friendly bump with her shoulder, and together they went into homeroom.

The rest of the school day proved uneventful,

except that when she dropped her eraser in math class, Corey went practically horizontal as he leaped out of his chair to retrieve it for her. The whole class laughed, even Ms. Kerry.

That evening, Alex finished her social studies reading just as her mother called her to set the table for dinner. It was a unit on economics, which other kids had complained was boring, but Alex secretly found fascinating. She loved learning about balancing budgets and learning terms like "supply and demand" and "opportunity cost" and "economies of scale."

As she descended the stairs, a sudden thought struck her. An amazing, incredible thought. It was the answer to her problems! She bounded down the rest of the stairs and found her parents talking together in low voices in a corner of the kitchen, their heads bent toward each other as though they didn't want to be overheard. When Alex came in they jumped back, almost guiltily.

What is the big secret? Alex wondered. She was no longer optimistic about it being a special Christmas surprise, but what else could it be? She pushed her curiosity aside for the moment—first things first. She skipped over to the cupboard and pulled out five dinner plates, and then pirouetted over to the table to lay them down, humming a little.

Her mother's eyes narrowed suspiciously. "Have you decided to cheer up, then, Alex?" she asked. "You've been doing a lot of dramatic sighing these past few days."

Alex smiled. "I know, sorry," she said. "I didn't realize how much our flights to Boston would have cost the family, so I shouldn't have assumed we could also afford to throw a party. I know that the opportunity cost of flying to Boston meant we would need to forgo the party, because to do both would have been prohibitively expensive for our family budget."

Coach nodded warily and handed Alex five napkins from the drawer.

"But here's the thing," said Alex, laying each napkin to the left of each plate. "What just occurred to me is, now that we're not flying to Boston, we'll suddenly have all that money back in the bank, right? So according to economic theory, the value of the resource we didn't use can now be applied to the next most valuable resource."

Her mother crossed her arms and lowered her chin, frowning at Alex.

"So," Alex continued, a bit more uncertainly, "what I was thinking was, maybe now we can? Have the party? Here? With all the money we saved? It wouldn't cost more than one-fifth of one ticket. Or one-fourth maybe." She trailed off in a whisper and looked first at her mother and then at her father.

Fathers are not supposed to roll their eyes, Alex thought. That was kind of a violation of the laws of nature. But she was pretty sure her father had just rolled his eyes.

"Alex, your mother and I have said we can't host your party," he said. "We haven't changed our minds. What we do with the family's finances is, frankly, not really your business. Your mother and I work hard for a living, and at keeping this family clothed and fed and reasonably happy and healthy. But we must make choices. And hosting a seventh-grade holiday party is not, I regret to have to say again, a top priority." He handed her the silverware.

Alex's heart sank. Despair and anger at her parents engulfed her. She practically flung the silverware down at each place setting and stomped out of the kitchen without a word. Did her parents *enjoy* ruining her life?

Dinner that night was another quiet and gloomy affair. Mr. and Mrs. Sackett seemed annoyed at the three Sackett kids. For what, Alex could not fathom. They were the ones who had destroyed Tommy's music career. And Ava's basketball career. And Alex's social life. No, correction. Her whole *entire* life. And on top of that, they were the reason there'd be no snow this Christmas. No one said much, and even Tommy pushed away his plate after only three helpings.

Finally Alex asked to be excused. Her siblings muttered the same.

"Dishes first," said Mr. Sackett.

Well, of course. When do we not *have to do the dishes?* Alex thought bitterly. She knew of *plenty* of kids who were never asked to do dishes. In fact, Charlotte had casually mentioned the other day that they had not one, but two different housekeepers. And once, Charlotte had gotten picked up from school by her father's driver. *Charlotte has probably never lifted a sponge in her entire life,* Alex thought as she rinsed a plate. But given her parents' sudden and utter lack of comprehension of what it was like to be in middle school, and how much things mattered, like not backing out of hosting a party after you've said you *would* host it, it seemed wise to keep these thoughts to herself.

"One moment before you go, kids," said Mrs. Sackett.

The dishes done, all three kids had started for the door, but now they halted.

"Mrs. Barnaby is going to need some help again at the day-care center on Sunday afternoon," said Mrs. Sackett.

"I have rehearsal at three," said Tommy quickly.

Mrs. Sackett smacked her brow. "Of course. I forgot. Well, at least I'll have Ava and Alex."

The twins exchanged outraged looks.

"The day care isn't usually open on Sundays, but the college is administering a big exam, and many of the staffers can't be available to watch people's kids," said Mrs. Sackett.

Alex was not inclined to say yes in light of how her mother had said no—again, and for no good reason—to her party. "I'm not sure," she said. "I might have plans."

"Me too," said Ava, who was clearly not feeling generous toward her mother either.

Coach put down his glass and stared at the twins. "You'll both help out," he said firmly.

Both girls started to protest, saw the look on his face, and closed their mouths again.

Moxy was under the table, where she'd been waiting for the possibility of scraps falling. Suddenly she streaked out and nosed open the swinging door of the kitchen, barking like crazy.

And then the front doorbell rang.

CHAPTER NINE

Ava was the first one to reach the front door. It was unusual to have a visitor at this time on a Friday night, ringing the front doorbell. Most people they knew just rapped on the side door leading to the kitchen, and it was too late for a salesperson. Maybe it was Corey again?

By this point Tommy and Alex had joined her. It struck Ava that they must also think this visitor was going to be worth coming out to see. She stood on tiptoe and peered through the peephole. Then she gasped.

"Who is it?" demanded Tommy, moving her firmly to one side so he could have a look himself. "No way," he said.

By now Alex was struggling to hip-check her brother out of the way so that she could look too, but without success. Tommy simply brushed her away with one of his strong forearms, unlocked the door, and flung it wide open.

A tall, good-looking, somewhat scruffy-faced young man stood on the stoop.

For a split second, Ava didn't recognize him. Then her jaw dropped.

"Uncle Scott!" shrieked Alex.

Uncle Scott set down the two bags he was carrying and opened his arms wide. The two girls barreled into him for a hug. Tommy gave him a half hug from the side, given that the girls were taking up most of the front stoop. Moxy was still barking, but now it was excited barking, as though she remembered him and just wanted to announce his arrival.

The three kids pulled him inside and closed the door. Moxy ran around them in a circle, showing off her sheepherding skills.

"Uncle Scott, what are you *doing* here?" asked Ava. "I thought you were backpacking through Asia!"

"That was *last* year," said Alex. "Weren't you just in Alaska, on a fishing boat?"

Tommy, who had been peering through the window next to the front door, spoke up before Scott had a chance to answer. "Where's that awesome little red sports car you used to drive, Uncle Scott? How did you get here?"

"I took a cab from the bus station, T," he said. "And that sports car turned out to be overrated."

By this time Mr. and Mrs. Sackett had emerged from the kitchen. They did not look surprised to see Scott. Ava realized they'd been expecting him. Scott disentangled himself from the girls, stepped forward, and kissed Mrs. Sackett on both cheeks, European-style, and then hugged Coach—somewhat stiffly, Ava noticed.

With a slight shock, she realized it had been at least two years since they'd seen him. They'd gotten the occasional postcard, always from far-flung places. She and Alex had mounted each of his postcards on the bulletin board between their beds in their old house. They'd collected at least two dozen. She wondered where those postcards were now. *Alex probably has them filed by date in a box somewhere,* she thought.

Uncle Scott was several years younger than Coach—the youngest of Coach's three siblings. Sometimes he looked more like a teenager than a grown-up. Ava took in his fashionably scruffy face, faded jeans, trendy sneakers, black T-shirt, and close-fitting jacket. Like Coach, he was ruggedly handsome, but more like a guy in an aftershave commercial than, well, a dad. All the Sackett brothers had slightly curly hair, but while Coach had green eyes, Scott's eyes were dark brown and shiny, like espresso coffee beans.

"Uncle Scott is coming to stay for a while," Coach said to the kids. "We've invited him to spend the holidays with us."

"Why didn't you *tell* us?" squealed Alex. "We haven't seen him—we haven't seen you in ages, Uncle Scott! Have you been traveling the world?" she asked him eagerly. "Do you have a girlfriend? What happened to that glamorous actress you were dating back when Ava and I were in fifth grade? Remember we went to see her in that movie where she played a dead body?"

Before Scott could answer, Tommy was also firing questions.

"Do you remember when you took me to game four of the World Series when the Sox beat the Rockies?" asked Tommy. "And how Mike Lowell and Bobby Kielty both hit home runs and I almost caught a ball? Maybe we can go to a Mavericks game while you're here. And did you hear we won State?"

While Tommy was recounting the final few moments of the Tigers' state championship win, Ava looked from Uncle Scott to her father and back again. Uncle Scott seemed a little ill at ease, and she wondered why. He had always had such an easygoing, relaxed personality. She remembered that Tommy had always looked up to Scott more like an older brother than an uncle, and no wonder. As the youngest of the four Sackett boys, Scott was the only one who'd stayed behind in Texas, even after Ava's grandparents had moved to Florida. But as far as she knew, that was just a place from which he'd had his mail forwarded. For as long as she could remember, he'd been something of a wanderer, traveling the world, never holding down a job for long. For the first time ever, she wondered if her father and Scott got along. Could it be possible that maybe they had quarreled? Why else would Coach not have mentioned that Scott was coming?

"Have you eaten dinner, Scott?" asked Mrs. Sackett.

"Yep, I just ate," said Scott. "I didn't want you to have to worry about my special eating plan on the very first night."

"Special eating plan?" repeated Mrs. Sackett. Ava thought she sounded way too polite and formal to be talking to her brother-in-law.

"Oh! Ha, yeah," said Scott with a little chuckle. "I'm Ayurvedic now. Still vegetarian, of course, but nowadays I don't eat eggs or dairy. Or nightshade vegetables, like tomatoes and peppers. Those toxic alkaloids affect my vibrational and physical channels in negative ways."

"I see," said Mrs. Sackett faintly.

"Hey, I'm a vegetarian now too!" said Alex. "Should I stop eating nightshade vegetables like you?"

Mrs. Sackett gave Alex a panicked look. Ava saw Coach slip his hand into her mother's and give it a little squeeze.

Scott laughed. "Maybe wait until you've gotten totally used to being a vegetarian, Alex," he said. He ran a hand through his already unruly curls. "I'm pretty beat. It's been a long day."

"Yes, you do look tired," said Mrs. Sackett. "We'll put you in the study. Tommy, you can carry his bags in there. Ava, run and get some clean sheets and a pillow. And don't forget a towel."

"Thanks so much, Laura," said Scott. "And Ava, don't bother with a pillow. I brought my own. It's kapok."

"What the—" Coach stopped and began again. "What is kapok?"

"Oh, it's made from the seed pods of sustainably harvested kapok trees," said Scott, with an apologetic smile.

Mrs. Sackett was looking a little worried, but she stepped over to the study and pushed open the door. "Well, there's a fold-out couch and a small bathroom just for your use. You'll find it quite a blessing most mornings in this household." She shot Alex a meaningful look. Alex had been taking such long showers in the morning that she'd used up the hot water on several occasions, so Mrs. Sackett had had to set strict time limits for her. "Oh, and Alex, you need to clean up that craft project that's all over the floor. What *is* it, anyway?"

"It's my Secret Santa gift for the Christmas party," explained Alex. "I have Rosa, and I'm making her a padded bulletin board."

"Still our artistic one, huh, Alex?" asked Scott with a smile.

Alex beamed and nodded, but then her expression clouded suddenly. "Although right now the status of this party is in serious jeopardy, because a certain mother has told a certain daughter that she is not allowed to host the party, which is basically resulting in the ruining of that certain daughter's entire life. But—"

"That's enough of that talk, Alex," interrupted Coach.

There was an awkward silence.

"And *speaking* of presents," said Alex, barreling through the silence obliviously, "you are the absolute best present giver in the family, Uncle Scott. Remember those metallic markers you gave me for Christmas when I was eight? They were so awesome. Did you bring us anything from—"

"Alex!" said Mrs. Sackett. "That's enough for tonight. Scott looks like he's ready to get some rest. You can talk to him tomorrow."

A few minutes later, the bed was made and Alex had cleared her bulletin board supplies from the floor of the study. Scott thanked Mrs. Sackett and waved good night to the rest of them. Then he went into the study and closed the door.

"How long is he staying?" asked Tommy.

"I'm beat too," said Coach with an exaggerated yawn, ignoring Tommy's question. "Think I'll head to bed."

"You kids should get to bed early tonight as well," said Mrs. Sackett, turning and walking quickly toward her and Coach's bedroom.

As she lay in her own bed that night, Ava couldn't stop thinking about Uncle Scott's sudden appearance. Her parents *must* have known he was coming. Scott's arrival must have been the reason their Boston trip got canceled. And why her parents had been so secretive recently, with those private phone calls and whispered conversations. But why hadn't they said anything? Why were they not answering the question about how long he was staying? And why were they being so polite to Scott? In the past, they'd always given him a hard time about his eating habits and crazy lifestyle, and he'd always taken their teasing with a good-natured smile. Now they were acting like he was a complete stranger.

Just before she fell asleep, she thought she

heard male voices murmuring somewhere. Her bedroom was directly above the study. Was her dad talking with Uncle Scott? She was too sleepy to decide if she was really hearing it or just dreaming. And then she fell asleep.

CHAPTER TEN

On Saturday morning Alex awoke to the faint sound of a car engine purring. She glanced at the clock: it was 6:37. Now what was going on?

A few minutes later she tiptoed through the empty kitchen and followed the sound out to the yard.

Her father, Scott, and Tommy were in front of the shed, working on an old, beat-up car. There were car parts everywhere.

"Morning, honey!" called Coach. He turned off his sander and wiped his brow.

"What are you doing? Whose car is that?"

"It's for your uncle," said Coach.

Scott finished polishing one of the hubcaps

and looked up at Alex. "Your dad picked this up for me and is helping me get it into good working order," he said. Alex could hear his appreciation in his voice.

Ava awoke to the sound of power tools. She glanced at the clock—6:55—and groaned. She sat up blearily. She was never one to wake up quickly. After a few minutes of listening to the clanking and banging, she realized the sounds must be coming from outside. What was going on?

By the time she managed to rally herself to get out of bed and pull on clothes, half an hour had passed. She made her way down to the kitchen and found Coach, Tommy, and Alex sitting around the kitchen table. Her mom had just come in from walking Moxy. Uncle Scott was wearing an apron and stirring something at the stove. It smelled strange and exotic, but wonderful.

"Morning, sunshine!" called Uncle Scott cheerfully. "Just in time for breakfast."

"Uncle Scott insisted on cooking this

morning," said Mrs. Sackett, hanging Moxy's leash on the hook.

"It's a South Asian–style porridge with carrots, peas, cumin, ginger, and turmeric!" said Uncle Scott. He ladled something brown and gloppy into a line of bowls.

"What was all the noise I heard?" asked Ava, raising her eyebrows at the porridge Scott carried to the table.

"They're restoring a used car," said Alex. "For Uncle Scott."

Ava looked from her mother to her father and back again. "Is Uncle Scott going to live with us from now on?" she asked.

"Sit. Eat your, uh . . . porridge," said her father. Once again he had ignored her question.

Ava slid into her chair and took a bite of the porridge. It was quite good. This was getting stranger and stranger.

The rest of the day passed, and all Ava's unspoken questions remained unanswered. How long was her uncle here? What had brought him here? Were her parents glad to have him or not? Uncle Scott was so busy helping Coach in the driveway and then offering to run to the health food store and prepare dinner for everyone, she didn't have an opportunity to ask him.

For dinner, he cooked a spicy stew, with rice and vegetables. She had to admit, it was delicious, whatever it was. Tommy had three helpings. But her parents continued to avoid any conversation related to Scott's stay. And Scott seemed to be going along with it, changing the subject whenever one of the kids tried to bring it up.

That night the twins tagged along to a movie with Tommy and Cassie. Ava was pretty sure their parents had forced Tommy to get them out of the house so they'd stop asking questions.

It was after ten o'clock when they pulled back into the driveway. Tommy turned off the engine and the three of them stayed in the car, peering at the house. Their parents' light was off.

"Uncle Scott's still up," said Tommy.

Ava nodded. She knew he was as curious as she and Alex were.

"Why do you think he's here?" asked Alex.

Ava shrugged. "I wish I knew," she said. "I feel like there's a story we haven't heard yet." She peered out the car window. "He just turned off his light."

"Should we go talk to him?" asked Alex.

Ava looked at Tommy. He nodded.

A few minutes later the three of them were standing outside the closed study door. Moxy had joined them, as though she sensed there was drama.

"Knock again," whispered Alex.

Tommy did, this time a little louder.

From inside they heard rustling and the creaking of bedsprings. "Come in, guys," came Scott's sleepy voice.

How does he know it's us? Ava wondered. It was almost like he was expecting them.

They all filed into the study. Uncle Scott had turned his light back on and was sitting up in bed. He smiled sleepily at them and patted the bed, inviting them to sit down. Moxy jumped up immediately.

"Sorry to wake you," said Tommy in a low voice.

"Hey, this is the best good night a guy could wish for," said Scott. "The world's three most awesome kids. And their awesome, if large, dog."

Now Ava remembered why she'd always loved Uncle Scott and been so charmed by him. Even as a tiny kid, she'd felt his warmth and his kindness and had constantly been showing him bugs she'd caught and baseball cards she'd collected when he visited.

They all settled in around Moxy. The bed was now very crowded. Ava could feel the lumpy bedsprings through the thin mattress. Not the world's coziest place to sleep.

"Let me guess. You want to know why I showed up like this out of the blue," Scott said.

They all nodded.

"Well, it was kind of sudden for me, too," he admitted. "I lost my job last week. I got laid off at the software company where I'd been working for a couple of months, over in San Antonio."

"I'm sorry," whispered Alex, her eyes round.

"Yes, well, it happens," said Scott. "I haven't exactly been Mr. Responsible since I graduated from high school."

"But you've done so many cool things!" protested Tommy.

"All that traveling," said Ava.

"Well, yeah, that was pretty cool," admitted Scott.

"That little red sports car," said Tommy wistfully.

"It was constantly in the shop," said Scott. "I traded it in."

"That glamorous actress girlfriend!" added Alex.

"She left me for a stock trader," said Scott with a shrug.

"So are you here to stay? Will you move in with us permanently?" asked Ava.

Scott smiled. "Probably not permanently, guys," he said. "But it may be awhile before I get on my feet again. Your parents are the most generous people ever. I hope you realize that."

None of them said anything. Ava thought about how her parents weren't letting her play basketball.

"I always thought you had the coolest life," said Tommy. "Traveling, seeing the world . . ."

"Listen, T," said Scott. "You're right that seeing the world is great, and I have no regrets about that. But I wish I had worked harder in school. Your dad set some pretty high standards for the rest of us—he got good grades, he was a great athlete, he won a college scholarship. I guess in a way I felt like I couldn't measure up to him, so I stopped trying. And I didn't apply to college. That I do regret."

The three of them were quiet, thinking about that.

"I've never been much good about saving for a rainy day. But now, thanks to your parents, I think I'll be able to swing going to college part-time. I'm good with computers, so hopefully I'll find a decent-paying job soon. I'm on a new path. A good one. But I couldn't have pulled this off without your parents' help."

"If they're helping you, why were they being so weird about telling us why you were here?" Alex asked.

"That's my fault," said Scott. "I asked them not to tell you why I was coming. I guess I was a little embarrassed about my situation, and I didn't want you guys to think badly of me."

"We would never—" Ava cried out.

"I know, I know," Uncle Scott said, patting her knee. "And it was silly of me, anyway—you guys are smart, and obviously you all were going to wonder what was up when I showed up on your doorstep. I shouldn't have put your parents in that position when they've done so much for me. Your mom has even been calling around trying to help me get interviews. So you guys should really stop being angry with them about that."

"It wasn't just that," said Tommy, "even though

that was part of it. They promised we could go to Boston, and my whole career was riding on it, and—"

"And nothing, champ," Scott interrupted. "I hear you're incredibly talented, and that your band is a hot ticket. It's not going to stop being that. Again, be mad at me, for being such a terrible planner. Because I'm guessing the reason you guys aren't going to Boston is that your parents used the money for your trip to help *me* out. They invited me to stay here until I could get back on my feet, and your dad bought that car so I'd have a way to get around."

That shut Tommy up.

"And you," said Scott, turning to Alex. "What's this I hear about you giving your mom the silent treatment because she won't let you have a Christmas party?"

"Oh, that," said Alex, the color rising in her face. "Well, yeah. I mean, I sort of forgot to mention the hosting part to my mom before I told my friends I would have it here at our house, and now they're making it into this massively important party with decorations and contests and food requests, and I haven't gotten up the nerve to tell them I can't host it and they're all going to ostracize me and—"

"Alex," said Scott, leaning forward and putting a hand to the side of her cheek. Her talking had sped up and her voice had grown shrill, which Ava knew was a sign that her sister was seriously stressing. Scott seemed to understand that too, but his gentle touch calmed Alex quickly.

"Look at me and tell me honestly. Do you *want* to host this party?"

"Of course! Well, sure, kind of. Actually, not really," she finally admitted. "It would be a ton of work, and planning, and cleanup and stuff. But I promised my friends. And I can't let them down."

"So use me as the reason," said Scott simply. "Tell your friends your uncle has suddenly shown up for a visit, and he doesn't like wild parties. Someone else is bound to step up and volunteer."

Alex blinked at him. "That's a brilliant idea," she said. "Why didn't *I* think of it?"

"And keep using words like 'ostracize,'" Scott added, grinning. "I like your style."

Alex beamed.

"And you, Ave? Is everything cool between you and your parents, or do you have an issue with them too?"

"I have an issue," said Ava.

"She really does have a reason to be mad," said Tommy loyally. "They're not letting her play basketball. Have you *met* her? If she can't play sports, she's going to spontaneously combust."

"I have ADHD," said Ava glumly. "I was diagnosed this year. And they think I need more structure and time to devote to my homework and stuff. They talked to the learning specialist at school, who told Mom that night practices are going to be 'disruptive.'"

"Hmm, I see," said Scott. He scratched his scruffy chin.

"The thing my parents don't seem to realize is that *not* playing a sport is making me less able to concentrate, not *more* able," said Ava. "I mean, like this dumb persuasive essay I'm supposed to write. I turned in my outline and everything, but I just can't seem to get fired up enough to write four pages about why we should have a longer lunch hour."

"Yeah, that does sound kind of tedious," agreed Uncle Scott.

"I just can't sit still and focus for two seconds on it. I need to run around. Studies have shown that. I mean, I haven't actually *read* any, but I'm pretty sure studies have shown it."

"Hmm," Scott said. "You sound like you want to persuade your parents to let you play, right?"

"Well, yes, but they won't listen because—"

"You want to *persuade* them." He emphasized the word.

"Yes."

"So why not make that a topic for a *persuasive* essay?"

Ava stared at him. It was such an obvious solution! "But I already submitted the outline," she said.

"So e-mail your teacher and see if you can change your topic. Go find your studies and use them. And write it in your essay. The best writing comes from feeling passionate about something, and you are obviously passionate about this subject."

Now it was Ava's turn to blink at Uncle Scott. "That's brilliant," she said.

"Of course it's brilliant," he said. "I really don't know how the three of you guys were able to function before I came back into your lives." He scooted back down into a reclining position, which caused Moxy to jump off the bed and shake herself, her collar jingling, and made Tommy topple to the side and almost fall off the bed. "Now beat it," he said, closing his eyes. "Your father is going to get me up early in the morning so we can finish working on the car. I need my beauty sleep."

The next morning Ava woke up and immediately turned on her computer to see if there was a message from Mr. Rader. There was. He was okay with her changing her topic.

"Yes!" she said out loud, and got dressed quickly.

When she got downstairs, Mrs. Sackett was pulling eggs out of the refrigerator. Butter sizzled in the pan. Strips of shiny bacon were already cooked and draining on a paper towel. Alex was emptying the dishwasher.

"Where's Uncle Scott?" asked Ava.

"He and your father have gone to the hardware store for more supplies," said Mrs. Sackett. "What he made yesterday was quite delicious, but I thought we'd have a more, um, traditional breakfast today."

Ava watched her mother crack an egg into

her coffee cup. "Mom," she said gently, nodding her head toward the coffee cup.

"What?" said her mother. "Oh, drats." She dumped the coffee into the sink. "What a day this is turning out to be," she said. "My clients just asked me to speed up the timing of their pottery order by a week. I just got a text from Michelle Cookson, who says she has a cold and can't help out at the day-care center this afternoon, so now I need to help Mrs. Barnaby find more helpers besides me to come with you to the day care, and—"

"Mom," said Alex. She stepped close to her mother and put a calming hand on the side of her cheek, just as Uncle Scott had done to her. "Sit. Have another cup of coffee. I'll finish making the eggs. Tommy can take Moxy out. Ava can text some of our friends and get them to meet us at the college and help oversee. You don't have to go. We'll handle it."

"You will?" asked Mrs. Sackett. Her eyes narrowed. "Why are you guys being so kind and helpful? I thought I was the worst mother in the world."

Alex gave her mother a bear hug. Ava joined her. Tommy's mouth was full, but he managed a grin and a thumbs-up.

"No, you're not," said Ava. "You're the best."

"I can't believe we got six kids to help out on a beautiful Sunday afternoon!" said Alex, as she and Ava surveyed the scene at the day-care center. Her heart was full of happiness. Plus, Corey was among the volunteers.

"Yeah, it's nice that so many of them rallied," agreed Ava.

"Hey, I heard you typing away all morning," said Alex. "What were you working on?"

"My essay," said Ava with a grin. "I'm almost done."

Alex beamed. "That's awesome, Ave," she said.

Lindsey and Emily were building a block castle with three little kids. Kylie was sitting at a table with a shy little boy, drawing pictures of horses. Corey and Jack were playing foam basketball with several little kids in the padded play area of the large room. Even Charlotte was there. She was overseeing two little kids at the finger-painting section. *She seems a little overdressed for babysitting,* Alex thought, glancing at Charlotte's flowing chiffon blouse and fashionable suede ankle boots.

"Mrs. Barnaby was psyched so many of us were coming," said Ava. "She told Mom she had so much confidence in us, she felt comfortable proctoring the test and letting us be in charge. So we're on our own until five."

"Incoming!" bellowed Corey. He was speed-walking across the room, holding a giggling two-year-old at arm's length.

Alex and Ava both laughed.

"Looks like Corey's got a diaper crisis!" said Alex.

Corey looked pleadingly into Alex's eyes. "I'll give you my entire college fund if you change this smelly diaper for me," he said to her.

Alex laughed again and took the little girl from Corey's grasp. "That won't be necessary," she said. "You were really nice just to volunteer to be here today. But I'll try to think of some way you can pay me back."

"Thanks, Alex," said Corey, and the smile he gave her made her knees go weak.

Hey! she thought. *I'm flirting! I thought I was terrible at flirting!*

Then she noticed Lindsey staring at them from across the room. She turned around quickly and hoisted the toddler up onto the changing table. What was Lindsey thinking? Lindsey and Corey seemed to have been acting pretty normal toward each other this morning—more normal than they'd seemed in a while—but Alex still felt very weird vibes whenever Lindsey caught Alex and Corey together, no matter how innocent the situation.

"When are you going to tell them about not hosting the party?" asked Ava in a low voice, after Alex had set the little girl down and they'd watched her race back to the basketball game.

Alex took a deep breath. "Now's as good a time as any, I guess," she said.

"Good luck," said Ava.

"Thanks," said Alex. She squared her shoulders and marched over to the block corner.

"Hi!" said Alex brightly. She sat down on the floor next to Emily and Lindsey, who were now watching the kids destroy the castle. "Thanks so much again for coming today," she said.

Emily smiled. "I love little kids," she said. "And two hours didn't seem like much to ask for a worthy cause."

Lindsey nodded. "Plus, it got me out of my weekend chores," she said.

"So I have something to tell you guys," said Alex. She swallowed, took a breath, and plunged on. "See, my uncle Scott showed up unexpectedly the other night. He's going to be staying with us through the holidays. We're not going back to Massachusetts anymore. And so here's the problem. With him staying at our house, I can't . . . I can't . . ."

Emily and Lindsey stared at her, wide-eyed.

" . . . I can't host the party."

The words hung in the air. Alex held her breath. She watched her friends exchange looks.

"Oh no," said Emily.

"Oh *no*!" echoed Lindsey.

"People have already started making Secret Santa gifts," said Emily.

"And they've already bought their ugly sweaters," said Lindsey.

With every sentence, Alex stomach sank more, and her shoulders hunched up a little higher. This was a social catastrophe from which she would never recover. She'd probably have her class presidency taken away. Could you be impeached from seventh-grade office? The warm, rosy feeling she'd had just a short time ago had now been replaced by gloom and dread. She had failed this social examination and would never recover. She would—

"Hey."

Her thoughts were interrupted by someone standing behind her. Emily and Lindsey, who were sitting facing Alex, looked up. Alex turned.

It was Corey.

He was holding a toddler cradled in each arm. Both kids were sweaty and red-faced from all the basketball, but happily slurping juice boxes. Alex recognized one of them as Dougie.

"We're just taking a little juice break," he explained. "What's all the fuss about?"

"It's the party," said Lindsey. "Alex just told us she can't have it at her house because her uncle is staying with them."

Great, now Corey will never speak to me again either, Alex thought.

"He's . . . he's not a fan of parties," Alex stammered out. Although that was so not true. Uncle Scott loved parties. But he had given her permission to say that.

Dougie held up his juice box and squeezed it. A stream of apple juice squirted the side of Corey's face.

"Hey, thanks, sport," said Corey.

Despite her agitation, Alex found herself laughing. He didn't even get mad at the kid. He was so good-natured!

"No one panic yet," said Corey. "I can ask my mom if we can host it at *our* house. I'm sure it's no big deal."

Emily and Lindsey sprang to their feet. Alex did too.

"That would be so amazing!" said Emily breathlessly.

"Here, hold him," said Corey, passing a kid to Emily. "And you hold him," he said with a mischievous smile as he passed Dougie to Alex. "Just watch out for that loaded juice box. This kid is trigger-happy."

He pulled a paper towel from his pocket and wiped off his face. Then he took out his phone and stepped to the side of the room, where it was a little quieter.

Alex noticed Charlotte making her way toward them. She had a swath of blue finger paint across her forehead. "Anyone know how to get finger paint out of suede boots?" she asked the assembled group.

Alex again wondered why on earth Charlotte had worn such nice clothes to volunteer today, but then she remembered how she'd run to put on a little makeup when Ava had told her that Corey was coming.

"I wonder if you could brush them—" she began.

"My mom said sure," Corey called out, glancing up from his phone.

Lindsey and Emily squealed with delight and jumped up and down.

Alex resisted a strong urge to dash over and hug him. But of course she couldn't do that. She settled on smiling gratefully at him. He caught her eye and smiled back. She darted a glance at Lindsey. Sure enough, Lindsey was staring keenly at the two of them. Alex felt her face get hot. "That's super awesome," she said to Corey.

"I owed you one," he said. "You changed that diaper for me. I think I got away with the easy part of the deal."

"The parents are here," called Ava, who was over near the sign-out area, helping tie a kid's shoes.

"Good," sighed Charlotte. "I need to go home and take a nap. Parenthood is exhausting."

CHAPTER ELEVEN

Ava finished her paper right after dinner on Sunday, a record for her. Usually she didn't finish assignments until super late the night before they were due. She pasted her essay into the online document according to Mr. Rader's instructions, and then opened her social studies textbook to get the reading done before bed. She smiled. Maybe she'd even let Uncle Scott read her persuasive essay. He would probably be proud.

Later that night, as she was trying to find a pair of clean socks to wear the next day, Uncle Scott knocked on her door. He was holding her essay in his hand. "Ave, this is fantastic," he said. "You're a really good writer."

Ava felt a surge of pride. Did he really think so? "It's no big deal," she said with a shrug.

"It's a big deal, Ave," he said, setting it down gently next to her bed. "It's clear that you worked hard on this."

In sixth period on Tuesday Mr. Rader announced he was passing back the graded essays. Ava was impressed. She appreciated teachers who graded things and got them back. She didn't always love the results she got, but it was so much better than the teachers who took forever to grade, keeping you in suspense way too long. Mr. Rader was efficient.

He put the essay facedown on Ava's desk and paused for a moment. "That was an excellent essay, Ava Sackett," he said. "I could sense the passion in your argument, and you presented it cogently and with great clarity."

"Thanks!" said Ava. She'd have to ask Alex what "cogently" meant.

"I'm especially pleased that you changed your topic," he continued. "We all write better when we're excited about what we're writing. And I understand you're an excellent basketball player. It would be great to have you try out for the team."

Ava stared at him. "*You're* the coach?" she asked. He smiled and nodded. How had she not known that? She'd been so wrapped up in fighting to play basketball, she supposed she'd just forgotten to ask who the coach was. Who knew it was her English teacher?

As soon as Mr. Rader had moved on, she peeked at the grade. Ninety-two! That was an *A minus*! She plunked it back down, her heart pounding. Had she imagined that grade? Or maybe she'd seen it upside-down, and the nine was really a six. Maybe it was a *sixty*-two. But then the two would be wrong. She peered at it again. The ninety-two was still there, and it was definitely not upside-down. She had trouble keeping herself from grinning big-time. She really had worked hard on it, though. She'd found half a dozen studies online that were written with super-academic language and hard to understand. But she'd laboriously put some of their conclusions into her own words, and she'd cited them in her bibliography the way Mr. Rader had instructed the class. One report had concluded that ADHD kids who participated in sports had greater self-efficacy, self-confidence, and happiness. She'd looked up "self-efficacy" and reworded it to say "an ability to believe in their own skills." Another said that teachers reported that kids in sports programs showed more persistence in the classroom. She'd reworded that to "they try harder in school." Another had described a decrease in attention-seeking behaviors. She'd reworded that to "they did not show off in class as much." She couldn't wait to show the paper to Mrs. Hyde. Maybe she could start by changing Mrs. Hyde's mind, and then move on to her parents!

As soon as the bell rang, she bolted out of class to find Mrs. Hyde. Luckily, her office was on the way to Ava's social studies class, and she found Mrs. Hyde sitting alone at her desk. Ava thrust her paper proudly into Mrs. Hyde's hands without even saying hello first.

Mrs. Hyde scanned it quickly, her smile broadening as she did so. "Why don't you share this with your parents, Ava?" she suggested, as soon as she'd finished.

Ava nodded. "I was planning to," she said. "It was kind of my uncle Scott's idea. He told me you always write better if you're allowed to choose a topic that you feel passionate about."

Mrs. Hyde nodded. "Your uncle Scott is a

wise person," she said. "And you've made a very compelling case in your own favor here. I mentioned to your parents that I was worried that the nighttime basketball practices would disrupt your routine, but I agree that it's more important for you to have an outlet for your energy. We can work together on a new study schedule if your parents agree to let you try out."

Yes! Ava thought. Mrs. Hyde agreed with her! All this time she'd thought Mrs. Hyde had made this dumb recommendation to her parents, but if she was an expert on ADHD, she'd certainly know what the research said.

Ava left the essay on her mother's pillow when she got home from school that afternoon. Her mom had said she'd be working late again at her pottery studio.

As no one besides Alex seemed to be home, Ava dribbled her basketball down the front stairs and around the corner, bouncing down the hall to the kitchen. As she passed the door of the study, she peered in to see if Uncle Scott was there, but he was definitely out.

Alex was sitting at the table, working on the bulletin board she was making for Rosa. "Ugh! That dribbling!" she exclaimed. "You know you're not supposed to dribble in the house!"

Ava picked up her dribble. "Where did Uncle Scott go yesterday and today?" she asked Alex.

"Daddy says he's 'pounding the pavement,'" said Alex, painting a long strand of ribbon with glue. "That means he's looking for jobs and distributing his résumé."

Ava nodded. "I hope he finds a job near us," she said.

"Me too," said Alex. "Hey, have you decided what you're going to make for Jack?"

Ava pursed her lips and frowned. She'd forgotten all about a present for Jack. "I can't think of anything," she said. "He told me he likes food, but I can't bake. Not like Coach, anyway." She pondered. "He does love dogs, though, and especially Moxy," she said.

At the sound of her name, Moxy, who was lying under the table at Alex's feet, thumped her tail loudly.

"Maybe you can make him a calendar with Moxy pictures for each month of the year!" suggested Alex excitedly. "I can help you!"

"I like that idea," said Ava. Having an artsy sister really comes in handy sometimes, she thought.

"Well, you can start by taking Moxy outside and taking some fun pictures of her," said Alex.

So that was what Ava did for the rest of the afternoon. She and Moxy walked around the neighborhood, and Ava posed her in different situations.

Later Uncle Scott called to say he had to meet someone for an interview and wouldn't be home for dinner. Between talking about the pictures she'd taken with Moxy and the lively dinner discussion about what sort of job Uncle Scott should get, Ava forgot all about her essay.

"He should become a television reporter, because he's so good-looking and has a nice broadcasting voice," said Alex. "I would know better than anyone about that, of course."

Ava rolled her eyes. Ever since Alex had been chosen to do a "Tomorrow's Reporters Today" segment on the local TV news station, she'd never let them hear the end of it.

"No way," Tommy scoffed. "He should open a sporting goods store. He's such a natural sales-man."

"I think he'd make a great coach," said Ava.

"Like Daddy?" asked Alex.

"No, I mean, like a coach for people about

how to live their lives," said Ava. "He's so good at giving advice."

"You mean a motivational speaker," said Tommy.

Ava caught Coach and Mrs. Sackett looking at each other, slightly amused. She supposed it was a little funny to think of Uncle Scott as someone who could give people advice about how to live their lives, considering that his had sort of fallen into disarray a little bit.

As the kids were finishing up the dishes, Coach and Mrs. Sackett went into the living room with cups of coffee and tea. Ava could hear them talking, but it was impossible to hear what they were saying because Tommy was blasting jazz while they cleaned up.

"Ave! Got a sec?" Coach's voice boomed from the other room, easily audible over the sound of Tommy's music. Ava liked to call it his "coaching voice." She tossed her dish towel onto the table and headed into the living room. Was she in trouble? She racked her brain to think which one of her teachers might have e-mailed her parents.

Her parents were sitting side by side on the couch. Her mother was holding Ava's persuasive essay. They both looked pleased. The only light in the room came from the twinkling colored bulbs on the Christmas tree, which cast a rosy glow on her parents' faces.

"Oh! You saw that, huh?" Ava grinned. "I forgot I left that for you to read."

"Great job, Ave," said Coach.

"Your father and I have talked about this business of you playing basketball," said Mrs. Sackett.

Ava lowered herself slowly into a chair, as though settling into a bath that might or might not be too hot. She tried her hardest not to get her hopes up.

"You make a very compelling case in favor of playing sports," continued Mrs. Sackett. "And you really did your research. I had no idea that so many experts were in favor of kids with ADHD participating in sports."

Ava nodded eagerly.

"We spoke to Mrs. Hyde earlier," said Coach.

Ava raised her eyebrows. Hopefully, Mrs. Hyde had been even more convincing about the benefits of kids with ADHD playing sports.

"And she agreed that we should give it a try

and see how this season goes for you," finished Mrs. Sackett.

Ava leaped out of her chair with a shriek.

"But!" Mrs. Sackett held up a hand to quiet her. "This is conditional upon you keeping your grades up. And making arrangements with Luke—well in advance so that he can plan his schedule—about setting up regular sessions with him, and—"

"Mom, I will, I will. I'll do all that, I promise!" said Ava, bouncing over happily and giving her a huge hug. Over her mom's shoulder, she sensed a movement in the doorway. It was Uncle Scott, who had just let himself in with his own key. He was nicely dressed in a jacket and tie, and he'd even shaved. He leaned against the door, winked at her, and gave her a thumbs-up.

Still hugging her mom, Ava winked back at him and gave him a return thumbs-up.

CHAPTER TWELVE

"It's Christmas Eve and it's fifty-seven degrees outside," said Alex. "I'm still not used to this."

She and Ava were standing side by side at the kitchen counter, peeling a huge mound of potatoes. Alex was wearing one of the many Christmas outfits she'd put together, but had tied on one of Coach's aprons to keep her clothes clean. Tommy had put on a playlist of jazzy Christmas carols, and Alex danced a little to "Jingle Bell Rock" as she peeled her potato.

"In some ways it's weird that it's so warm outside," agreed Ava, "but in other ways it's super awesome. I played full-court basketball for two hours outside today." She dropped a peeled potato into the bowl between them and picked up the next potato. "Although I will admit that it was odd to buy our Christmas tree from a guy wearing shorts and a T-shirt." She surveyed her sister's outfit, black leggings and a red sparkly tunic. "I see you went with snappy festive this evening," she said.

"Yes!" said Alex, happy that her sister remembered. "Although Coach's orange apron isn't exactly part of the look."

"You look like an Ashland Tiger," said Ava with a grin.

"Well, you look cute too," said Alex, and she meant it. She was pleased to see that Ava had made an effort at getting dressed up for the evening. She had on one of the two skirts she owned, and had borrowed Alex's green cardigan with the beaded collar, which she was wearing over a plain white T-shirt. Not what Alex would have paired it with, but definitely an improvement over Ava's normal choice of football jersey.

"Oh, and by the way—how are our Secret Santa presents coming along?" asked Ava.

Alex cocked an eyebrow. "*Our* presents, huh?" She slipped her potato into the bowl and put a hand on her hip. "I finished Rosa's present days ago. *Your* present for Jack is coming along," she said. "I've downloaded the software, chosen the template, laid out most of the pictures, and entered in most of our friends' birthdays. But I need you to take two more pictures of Moxy, for December and June. Maybe you can take a picture of her wearing reindeer antlers for December, and put a pair of sunglasses on her for June."

"Wow. That's a great idea," said Ava, looking genuinely impressed. "Sometimes I think you got double the creativity genes and I got none."

Alex narrowed her eyes at her sister, but she was secretly pleased by the compliment.

"I'll do that first thing tomorrow, promise," said Ava, looking guilty. "You're so awesome to help me with it."

"First thing tomorrow is Christmas morning," Alex reminded her. "Just do it the day after. Then we can bring it to the printing place and have them print it out. You get to wrap it, at the very least." *At least she appreciates what I'm doing,* Alex thought. And she'd actually really enjoyed making the calendar. She loved doing stuff like that.

"I'll wrap both gifts, I promise," said Ava.

They heard a knock at the front door, and Moxy started barking her head off.

"That must be Coach Byron," said Alex. "And Jamila and Shane." Coach and Mrs. Sackett had invited Coach Byron, one of the Tigers' assistant coaches, and his kids over for Christmas Eve dinner.

"I think I love Christmas Eve even more than Christmas," said Ava dreamily. "It's that feeling of being on the verge of wonderfulness."

Alex agreed.

As the nine of them settled around the dining room table, Alex looked around, still feeling happy and excited. Shane and Jamila were all dressed up, Shane in a little bow tie and Jamila in a sparkly Christmas dress. Ava brought in a bowl of vegetable stew, and Mrs. Sackett set down the best part of the whole dinner—popovers. Uncle Scott was still looking clean-shaven, and he'd put on a pressed white shirt and a skinny purple-and-yellow tie.

Alex could sense that Scott and her parents were really getting along well and enjoying one another's company. Scott had even helped Coach with the Christmas baking earlier in the day, although Coach had finally blown up and insisted that they have their traditional Christmas Eve meal with a couple of special dishes for Scott, not the other way around.

They're acting like brothers again, Alex thought. *I guess Uncle Scott's grace period after losing his job is over!*

Tommy nudged Shane, who was sitting to his left. "You're going to like those popovers, pal," he said. "I'm good for at least three of them."

Shane licked his lips and stared, his eyes shining.

Uncle Scott dinged his glass, rose from his chair, and cleared his throat. "I'd like to propose a toast," he said.

Everyone grew quiet.

"To my big brother, Mikey, and his fantastic wife, Laura. I want to thank you guys for your offer to help me during this, uh, transitional time in my life. You're blessed with three amazing kids, and you've done an amazing job raising them. I know I haven't been the easiest kid brother, and I know I've caused our mom and dad a lot of sleepless nights."

Coach chuckled and swiveled his gaze upward as if to say, *You said it, not me.*

"But you've always been an inspiration to me, and—" Scott's voice got a little thick.

Alex looked more closely down the table. Was that a tear in her uncle's eye?

He finished quickly. "So Merry Christmas, everyone. And just, well, thanks."

He sat down abruptly. He blew his nose on his napkin, but no one reprimanded him.

Tommy, who was leaning closer and closer toward the roast beef sitting in the center of the table, broke the spell. "So can we eat now?" he asked. "Shane and I are starving here, people."

Everyone laughed.

Alex felt a jab in her rib cage. Ava leaned in to whisper in her ear.

"I feel really, really guilty right now," said Ava. "After how mad I was at our parents for saying I couldn't play. Having Uncle Scott here kind of puts things in perspective."

"I feel bad too," Alex whispered back. "I can't believe how upset I was that Mom wouldn't let me have the party here. Now that I don't have to host it, I'm realizing it would have been my worst nightmare. I would have been so worried about everyone having a good time, and keeping the punch bowl filled, and restocking the food, that I wouldn't have had one second to enjoy the party. It's so much less stressful just attending."

Ava nodded. "And your stress about the party would have stressed out all the rest of the family too," she said. "So we'll all be happier."

After Coach Byron and his kids left, and the kitchen was all cleaned up, with all the dishes put away, the six Sacketts listened to a beautiful piano rendition of "O Holy Night."

Uncle Scott had donned Mrs. Sackett's orange apron, and Alex wondered how he managed to look so hip.

"This is a really nice version of my favorite carol," said Uncle Scott. "Who's the artist?"

Tommy grinned. "Me," he said.

"No way," said Uncle Scott. "You're a serious talent, T!" He gave Tommy a big hug. Tommy seemed pleased.

"Mom, Dad," said Alex. "I have something to say."

Maybe it was something in her tone of voice, but everyone stopped hugging and chatting and looked over at her.

"I feel really bad that I was kind of annoying about demanding to have the party," she said. "I know how hard you guys work, and in retrospect, it really wasn't the end of the world, or my social life, not to have the party here."

Mrs. Sackett smiled and reached out to tousle her hair. "Thanks, honey," she said. "Believe it or not, it made me feel really bad to say no to you. But sometimes being a mom can be hard."

Ava cleared her throat. "I want to say I'm sorry too," she said. "About being so sulky with you guys when you said I couldn't play basketball. I know you had my best interest in mind. What I should have done is talked it over with you, instead of just being mad and slamming doors and stuff."

Coach put an arm around her waist and gave her a big squeeze. "Well, you ended up advocating for yourself in a pretty mature fashion, Ave," he said.

Tommy cleared his throat. "Okay, okay. Gee, how did this evening suddenly get so sappy? I guess I should admit that not going to that party in Boston wasn't the end of the world for me, either. Especially since now we get to hang out with Uncle Scott this week.

What you're doing for him is pretty cool."

Coach and Mrs. Sackett looked at each other, surprised.

"I told them why I was here," Scott jumped in. "And how I asked you not to tell them—I realize now that wasn't fair to you."

Mrs. Sackett let out a huge sigh of relief.

"We didn't like keeping secrets from you guys," Coach said. "But we wanted to respect Scott's wishes, and we understood why he didn't want you to know he'd lost his job."

"And we didn't want to involve you in our family budget. But we should tell you that everything is fine—we're setting aside more money so we can all go to Boston next summer," said Mrs. Sackett. "And Alex, maybe with a little more notice, we can host a party in the spring sometime."

"That would be awesome!" said Alex. "And while we're on the subject of admitting to being annoying—I also just wanted to say I'm sorry I wasn't very gracious about working at the day-care center. It was actually really fun, and it made me feel good to help out."

"That's so nice, Alex," said Mrs. Sackett. "Mrs. Barnaby reported that you and your friends did a fantastic job, and that the kids have all requested that it be a regular thing!"

Alex and Ava both gulped.

"And I'm glad you think helping out is fun, because I've signed us all up to volunteer at a soup kitchen tomorrow."

"Tomorrow? But it's Christmas!" exclaimed Alex.

Uncle Scott cleared his throat loudly.

"I mean, wow. Great. That sounds like a plan!" said Alex brightly.

"I'm cool with that," said Tommy.

"Yep, me too," said Ava.

The next morning, after a big breakfast of gingerbread waffles (a delicious new experiment of Coach's) and fresh fruit salad, they all filed into the living room to open presents. Ava got a San Antonio Spurs jersey—just what she'd wanted. Tommy got a gift card to his favorite music store. Alex got the new outfit she'd been drooling over for weeks.

"How did you guys know this was what I wanted?" she asked.

"You did leave the catalog lying around with the page folded down and the outfit circled," Ava pointed out.

"Did I?" Alex asked innocently.

Tommy threw a bow at her.

Even Moxy got a present—a huge bone, straight from the refrigerator. She clamped her jaws around it and trotted over to Mrs. Sackett's newly cleaned rug, where she began gnawing away. Mrs. Sackett closed her eyes and turned away from the sight.

Uncle Scott left the room and reappeared with a slightly rumpled brown shopping bag. "I, uh, didn't have time to wrap," he said, "but I hope you guys like these. I got them last time I was overseas."

Tommy got a funky-shaped Egyptian string instrument that came with a bow and made a lovely, eerie sound. Alex got a Bedouin jeweled scarf. Ava got three different soccer team pennants, each in a different, strange-looking language.

"That's Arabic, Hebrew, and Urdu," said Scott.

"Whoa," said Ava. "These are way cool. Thanks, Uncle Scott."

Tommy gave each of the girls a snow globe. "So

you'll remember what snow looks like," he said.

"Hey," said Coach. "I distinctly remember it snowing here at *least* twice during my childhood."

"Not me," said Uncle Scott. "Can't remember the last time it snowed around here."

Tommy snorted. "The only snow we're going to see is inside those snow globes, Coach."

Ava and Alex always exchanged the last presents. It was something of a Christmas tradition in the house.

Alex opened her present from Ava. It was a new charm for her bracelet.

"What is it?" she asked, frowning.

"It's a baby rattle," said Ava. "To remind you of our stint at the day-care center."

Alex giggled. "Open yours," she said.

Ava tore the paper off her gift from Alex. It was a foam ball and indoor mini hoop.

"So you'll stop bouncing that infernal basketball in the house," said Alex.

"Ava's been dribbling in the house?" said Mrs. Sackett.

Ava glared at her twin.

CHAPTER THIRTEEN

The day of the party, Alex knocked on Ava's door and pushed it open. Ava was standing in the middle of her room, looking extremely uncomfortable in a large, lumpy ski sweater.

"You look . . . cute!" said Alex brightly.

Ava frowned and tugged at the neckline. "I hate wool. This sweater is so itchy. I feel like I'm crawling with ants."

Alex giggled. "Look! Uncle Scott got the lights to work on my sweater!" She pushed the button and the snowflakes began twinkling.

"That's hilarious!" Ava said.

"Thanks." She sat down on Ava's bed. "I'm really nervous about this party," she admitted. "I just don't know what to do about the Corey and Lindsey situation. I think he likes me, but every time he and I get within ten feet of each other, Lindsey seems to pop up out of nowhere. I just don't know if she's okay with this, and I don't want to lose her as a friend."

"Listen, Al," said Ava. She put a hand on her sister's shoulder and quickly took it off again, perhaps grossed out by the feel of the scratchy artificial fibers. "I think you should just talk to Lindsey straight out. Ask her what she's thinking. It's not really fair of her to like another guy but keep you and Corey from liking each other."

Alex sighed. "You're right. I'll try to talk to her."

"Hey, you twins!" bellowed Tommy from downstairs. "If you want a ride to your party, you'd better be down here quick!"

Even though Corey's house was in walking distance, Alex had declared that she absolutely could not be seen in public wearing her ugly sweater. "We'd better get going," she said. "Did you wrap the Secret Santa presents?"

Ava reached behind her bed and picked two misshapen packages off the floor, one large and one medium. "Yep," she said proudly.

Alex winced a little as she looked at the wrapping job Ava had done. Alex loved wrapping presents, getting the corners just right and the paper creased just so. Ava clearly did not share her enthusiasm. The bulletin board Alex had made for Rosa was wrapped in thick, shiny paper that Ava hadn't properly creased. It had visible pieces of tape and a sad ribbon that Ava had attempted, unsuccessfully, to curl. *Let it go,* she said to herself. "Looks great!" she chirped brightly, and the two hurried down to find Tommy.

Tommy dropped them off, and the girls surveyed Corey's house. It was large—three stories—and a wide flight of stairs led to the front entrance.

"Corey said the party would be in his basement, but I'm not used to Texas houses having a basement aboveground," remarked Ava.

Alex shivered. She seemed too nervous to comment. Ava knew she was stressing about Corey and Lindsey. Or possibly it was the fact that the weather had definitely turned colder since this morning.

Corey's mom greeted them at the front door. "Ava!" she said. "This must be your twin sister!"

Ava had met both of Corey's parents before, of course, as they'd come to most of their football games. She introduced Mrs. O'Sullivan to Alex. Alex, who was usually pretty comfortable around adults, stammered out a nervous hello.

"Oh, don't you two look adorable!" she gushed, pulling Alex and Ava into the house. "Everyone's downstairs, but I insist on taking a picture!"

Mr. O'Sullivan came around the corner, carrying a tray full of cheese and crackers. "Hello, Ava," he called. "And you must be Alex! Great sweaters!"

Alex laughed, but Ava could hear a nervous edge to it.

"I'm just replenishing some of the food down there!" he said, heading toward the basement. Ava could hear music playing and voices murmuring.

"Stand here, in front of the trophy case," Mrs. O'Sullivan commanded the girls.

"Mom! Dad!" Corey had come up the stairs at the sound of the doorbell. "Enough already!"

Ava laughed when she saw Corey. He had on an electric-purple sweater vest. The way it clashed with his red hair was, well, hideous. But even more so, she noticed, his face had gone as red as his hair. Was he embarrassed by his parents?

"You don't need to take a picture of everyone," said Corey to his mother, through gritted teeth.

"Too late!" she said with a laugh.

"Come on down, you guys," said Corey to Alex and Ava. "Dad, I got that," he said, and took the tray out of his father's hands. "Thanks, though."

As they headed downstairs, Corey apologized for his parents. "They've been brutal ever since my brother went off to college and I've been the only kid," he explained. "That would have been the third trip my dad made down the stairs in half an hour, if I'd let him go."

Ava smiled. She was glad Alex liked Corey. He was nice, and willing to be seen in public wearing an ugly sweater vest with snowmen all over it.

At the bottom of the stairs, Corey set the tray down on a table that was already overloaded with food and gestured around. "You can stick your presents over in that pile," he said. "And in there we have a pool table and Ping-Pong and stuff." Through the open doorway Ava spotted

Jack and Kylie playing a heated game of Ping-Pong. She saw Charlotte at the pool table and did a double take at the sight of her sweater. It appeared to have actual Christmas ornaments hanging from it, which she guessed were probably pom-poms made of yarn. Ava saw two kids with their backs to her shooting baskets on an electronic basketball game complete with scoreboard and buzzer. It was a dream basement, as far as Ava was concerned.

"Your decoration committee did a great job," said Alex.

Corey rolled his eyes. "That would be my mom," he said.

Ava hadn't paid much attention to the decorations, but she did so now. Strings of lights sparkled, and garlands of mistletoe were strung along the walls. Fun dance music played, but not deafeningly so. There seemed to be way more people than Ava expected. Lindsey and Emily, the main party planners, must have increased the guest list significantly. Nearly everyone wore an ugly sweater, and many had accessorized with ugly socks, pants, and headbands with reindeer antlers.

"O'Sullivan, you're up next!" yelled Jack from

the doorway. "I just demolished Kylie." His eyes fell on Ava and he waved.

Ava waved back, pointed at his sweater, and gave him a big thumbs-up. Jack's sweater was green with a huge reindeer face on the front, and it was way too small for him.

As soon as Corey had joined Jack at Ping-Pong, Ava felt Alex tugging on her arm. "There's Lindsey," she whispered. "Did you see how she was staring at us as we came down the stairs? I don't think I can do it, Ave. I'm too nervous to talk to her about Corey."

"You can do it, Al," said Ava. "Go now, before you lose your nerve. I'm off to go annihilate Jack in Ping-Pong, as soon as he's beaten Corey."

A little while later, Emily yelled "Secret Santa time!" Lindsey stopped the music, and everyone gathered around in a big group near the pile of presents. Emily plunked a Santa hat onto Corey's head, which Alex couldn't help but notice made him doubly adorable. Even if his red curls did clash with the hat.

One by one everyone opened their gift from

their Secret Santa. Alex held her breath when Rosa opened the bulletin board she'd made for her. But Rosa seemed genuinely pleased by it. Everyone else complimented Alex on her awesome craft skills, which made her feel good. She had to admit, she'd done a pretty good job with the quilting and the diagonal ribbons. She'd chosen the complementary shades of orange and gray carefully and had added a dash of aqua for contrast.

Jack really liked his Moxy calendar from Ava, too, although he eyed Ava suspiciously and asked her if she'd really put it together all by herself.

"Of course!" said Ava with mock indignation. "All it takes is a little Internet expertise, the right camera . . . and Alex Sackett as your twin sister."

Everyone laughed at that, and that made Alex feel even happier.

Ava's Secret Santa was Lindsey, and her gift was a collage of pictures from Ava's football season. In the middle was a crowd shot of everyone wearing their pink T-shirts in support of Ava being on the team. Ava seemed genuinely touched. "This is really great," she said to Lindsey.

When it was Logan's turn to open his present,

he pulled out a bright-orange, misshapen-looking length of knitting. "Uh, wow!" he said, looking around. Then he glanced at the card and his eyebrows shot up. "Thanks, Charlotte."

Charlotte smiled shyly. "I made it myself," she said. "I taught myself how to knit by looking at videos online. I had a little trouble casting on, and keeping the stitches even, and I know it's not long enough for a scarf, but I figured you could maybe use it as a pot holder."

Everyone laughed, even Charlotte.

"What do you give to the guy who has everything?" Corey remarked.

But Logan acted like he was really happy to have it. Alex wondered if maybe he might like Charlotte. She filed that away for future pondering.

"Hey, Alex didn't get one," said Emily.

"Oh, right," said Corey. He held out a present for Alex. "Almost forgot this."

Is he blushing? Alex wondered. With a jolt she realized that Corey must be her Secret Santa. The present was long and narrow, about the size of a TV remote, but it felt smooth through the lumpy wrapping. Clearly Corey had wrapped this himself, without any help from his mother.

Even Ava was a better present wrapper. Slowly she pulled off the paper.

It was a nameplate, made of triangular-shaped wood that would allow it to stand on a desk. The carved letters weren't perfectly formed or anything, but they were definitely readable: MADAM PRESIDENT.

"Awww!" said several guys. Someone gave Corey's shoulder a playful shove.

Corey reddened again.

Alex realized it must be inconvenient to be a redhead sometimes, because even though your hair is a thrilling color, redheads seemed prone to very visible blushing.

"I had to make *something* in wood shop," Corey muttered with a shrug.

"Look, Al, the bottom looks like it slides off," Ava said, leaning in to look.

Alex looked. Sure enough, the bottom of the nameplate was a different wood from the top. She slid the top and bottom in opposite directions, and the bottom came off, revealing a hollow interior. Inside was the hair clip she'd admired in the thrift shop that time they'd all gone together. She pulled it out. Now it was her turn to blush.

"Hey, I thought everyone was supposed to *make* their gifts!" said Rosa.

There was an awkward silence. Then Jack stuck a paste-on bow on Corey's Santa hat, and Ava jumped up and clasped her hands.

"Isn't it time for the sweater-judging contest?" she asked.

Alex shot her a grateful look.

Charlotte won the contest. Her sweater, with its protruding, round yarn pom-poms made to look like ornaments, was the hands-down favorite. Emily and Lindsey presented her with her prize: an ugly knitted Christmas hat. It had a pointy top that was attached to a long string, on the end of which was a huge yarn pom-pom that practically matched those on Charlotte's sweater.

"How could we not give it to you?" Emily laughed. "It was made to be worn with your sweater!"

Charlotte put on the hat and beamed. She even managed to look chic in her hat and sweater outfit. *Only Charlotte,* Alex thought.

"Hey," said a low voice next to her.

It was Lindsey. Alex jumped.

"I have something for you," said Lindsey, and she pulled Alex to the back of the group where they wouldn't be seen. Lindsey held something out to her but kept it hidden, so anyone observing them wouldn't know what it was.

Alex gulped. Was Lindsey going to give her a letter saying she was never going to speak to her again?

She held out her hand, trying not to let it shake, and Lindsey pressed something scratchy into her palm.

It was a sprig of mistletoe.

"Uh, thanks?" said Alex, feeling seriously confused.

Lindsey gestured toward Corey, who was across the room, jokingly strutting with Jack like male models on a runway.

"Just go talk to him, why don't you?" said Lindsey. Her expression was open and encouraging, not angry.

"To—to who?" Alex stammered out, although of course she knew who Lindsey meant. Also, she knew grammatically she should have said to whom, but she didn't want to sound like a big jerk.

"Duh, Corey. Anyone with a pair of eyes can see you two like each other." Lindsey sighed, crossed her arms, and leaned against the wall. "Okay, okay, I admit that I was a little weirded out by it when I first realized. I mean, even though I am so over him, he was still my first crush and the first guy I ever went out with. And it bothered me a lot when he broke up with me when I wasn't expecting it. That's why I kept trying to come between you guys whenever I saw you together. But I get that that's not fair, especially because I really do like Johnny."

"You really don't mind?" asked Alex.

"I really don't," said Lindsey. "So go *talk* to the guy."

And Lindsey turned and walked away, with Alex still clutching the sprig of mistletoe.

Someone turned the music back up, and people actually began dancing. Alex looked wildly around for Ava, desperate to tell her what Lindsey had said. But she was dancing with Jack and Kylie. She'd taken off her itchy sweater and was just wearing her Spurs jersey, looking much more comfortable.

Air. That's what she needed. She needed to get outside and gulp some fresh air. But the thought of walking up the stairs past Corey's parents was extremely unappealing.

Ha! There was a corridor leading to a door, and the door led straight outside. Now she was really happy that Texas basements were actually situated on the first floor.

Alex slipped out of the main room, headed past the washer and dryer, and tried the knob. It was open, and it led into the O'Sullivans' back-yard.

The air had grown even colder, but it felt nice after the heat and noise of the party. Alex was happy she had her sweater on. She sat down on the low stone wall and breathed.

The door to the house flew open and Corey stepped outside. "Alex!" he said, hurrying to her side. "Are you okay? I saw you leave, and . . . are you sick?"

Alex sprang to her feet, flustered all over again. "Oh, no, sorry," she said, weirdly out of breath. "I just felt like I needed some air is all." She shivered, whether from cold or from excitement at standing so close to Corey, she had no clue.

"You're shivering," said Corey, coming even closer to her. Now she could see how long his eyelashes were. And how well his broad shoulders filled out his too-tight, patterned sweater vest. "What's that in your hand?" he asked her, and gently put his hand over hers. The one that was still clutching the sprig of mistletoe. The other hand was in her pocket, clutching the hair clip.

He drew her hand up to his face so he could see that it held mistletoe. With a little smile, he kept gently tugging at her hand until it was raised up high, so that they were standing under the mistletoe.

Oh my gosh, he's going to kiss me, thought Alex. Now she really did feel faint. She didn't know what to do with her mouth, whether to close her eyes, whether to—ACK! Panic shot through her system and she squeezed her eyes shut. A cold, feathery chill fell upon her face.

Her eyes flew open. Corey's face was close to hers, but there were white snowflakes swirling between them. She gasped. "It's snowing! Look, it really is!"

Corey looked up at the white snow falling from the black sky.

The window in the kitchen, which looked out over the backyard, flew open. Corey's mom poked her head out. "It's snowing!" she called to them, somewhat unnecessarily. "Your father is running down to tell the rest of the kids! He wants to take a group picture!"

Alex and Corey looked at each other. They both started to laugh.

At that moment, the door leading from the basement burst open. All the kids at the party streamed into the backyard. They hadn't needed prompting from Mr. O'Sullivan. They twirled and jumped around in the dancing white flakes, which were thick and heavy, and melted as soon as they hit the ground. Still, it was snow.

Jack and Xander grabbed Corey and dragged him away.

Ava joined Alex and they stood, watching the feathery flakes fall. "It's not going to stick, of course," said Ava.

"I suppose not," said Alex. "But it's still a magical night."

Ava looked at Alex and cocked her head. "How magical?"

Alex blushed. "Pretty magical."

Ready for more
ALEX AND AVA?

Here's a sneak peek at the
next book in the **It Takes Two** series:

Twice
the Talent

So it really happened just like that?" Alex Sackett asked.

"Absolutely," answered Charlotte Huang. "Mom was like, this kitchen renovation is driving me crazy, I just can't take it anymore, and the next thing I knew we were on a plane to the Bahamas."

"That sounds amazing," said Rosa Navarro, a dreamy look in her brown eyes.

It was a Tuesday afternoon, Christmas break was over, and Alex and her friends Charlotte, Rosa, Emily, Lindsey, and Annelise were hanging out at Emily's house. They had piled into Emily's cozy bedroom. Alex sat on the floor, clutching a throw pillow.

Sometimes it was hard to believe that she and

her family had only moved to Ashland, Texas, a few months ago. It hadn't been easy to leave her life and friends in Boston behind—but here she was, with all new friends, laughing and talking like she'd known them forever.

"What's amazing is your tan, Charlotte," said Annelise. "I get so pale during the winter."

"Not to mention freezing," said Lindsey with a shiver. "I'd love to be on a sunny beach right now."

Alex held back a smile. It was forty-nine degrees out, which was chilly for Texas, but downright balmy for a winter day in Boston.

Emily, the girl in the group Alex felt closest to, noticed her amused expression.

"I bet this is beach weather in Boston, right, Alex?" she teased.

"Exactly," said Alex, playing along. "Back home everyone's wearing flip-flops and building snow castles by the ocean."

"Ooh, we built this fabulous sand castle at the beach by our hotel," said Charlotte, scrolling through her phone to find the photos. "Mom hired a sand castle architect and he helped us. It had, like, twenty towers and a stable and everything."

Alex raised an eyebrow. "Is there really such a thing as a sand castle architect?" she asked. Although as soon as she asked the question, she knew she shouldn't have been surprised. Charlotte's family had two housekeepers and a driver. Hiring someone to help build your sand castle was probably no big deal.

"Yeah, he worked with the hotel," Charlotte replied, and then she frowned. "I can't find it! Oh, wait, here's that shot from the Christmas party!"

Everyone gathered around Charlotte to look, even though they all had tons of photos from the party on their phones. They'd held an Ugly Sweater party on the Saturday after Christmas, and it had probably been Alex's best night in Ashland so far.

The photo on Charlotte's screen was a group selfie of everyone in their ugly sweaters, mugging for the camera. There was Alex, laughing with her arm around her twin sister, Ava. They looked identical except for Alex's long, wavy hair and Ava's shorter, sporty haircut.

Next to Alex was Emily, sticking her tongue out, and Lindsey, who was posing like a supermodel. There were boys in the photo too, but the one who caught Alex's eye was Corey O'Sullivan. He wore a silly grin on his face and a Santa hat on top of his red hair.

"That was such a fun night," said Rosa. "Although I'm glad I won't have to wear that ugly sweater ever again!"

"The sweaters are what made it a fun night," Emily pointed out.

"And the Secret Santa exchange," added Annelise.

Lindsey got a mischievous twinkle in her eyes. "That was a sweet gift that Corey gave you, Alex," she said quietly. "You know, you never told me if you and Corey used that mistletoe."

Alex felt her face get hot, and she knew she must be bright red. She and Corey had almost kissed that night, under the falling snow, but she hadn't told anybody about it—not even Ava. She wasn't about to tell anyone in this room.

Part of the reason was that everything with Corey was super complicated. She had developed a crush on him right away when she first met him, but then she learned that Lindsey liked him too, so she backed off. Corey and Lindsey went out, but broke up. Then Lindsey started liking Johnny Morton, an eighth grader. That led to the Christmas party, where she gave Alex mistletoe and told her she should go talk to Corey.

And Alex had talked to Corey, outside, and they almost kissed—until the snow started to fall, which didn't happen too often in Texas. Everyone had streamed outside, and the moment was over. But it had still been a magical moment, and it had been hers—just hers and Corey's.

"Mistletoe? What about Alex and Corey and mistletoe?" Annelise asked eagerly.

"Hey, didn't we come here so that you guys could work on your Variety Show routine?" Alex asked, trying to change the subject.

Her ploy worked. "That's right!" Emily said, jumping up off her bed. "The show is only three weeks away and we've barely started practicing."

"Or working on our costumes," said Rosa. "We've got to think of something that will go with the Wild West theme."

"So what are you guys doing?" asked Alex. The Variety Show seemed to be a big deal at Ashland Middle School. It was just about all anyone could talk about now that the holidays were over.

Annelise smiled. "We're going to do a dance, like we did last year. You should dance with us!"

"Come on, you know I have two left feet," Alex said. "Besides, as student council president I volunteered to work backstage."

"That makes sense. I can just see you with a clipboard, organizing everybody back there. It can get pretty hectic," Emily remarked.

Lindsey shook her head. "You could still dance with us. It's a pretty easy dance. Charlotte's new, and she picked it up right away. Here, I'll show you."

Lindsey jumped up and kicked a pillow out of her way. Then she played a song on her phone. It was a country song that Alex had never heard before, something about a broken heart.

Lindsey started moving her hips from side to side and tracing a heart in the air with her fingers. Emily, Rosa, Charlotte, and Annelise joined her. It was close quarters and the girls kept bumping into one another. They looked a little stiff, and frankly, Alex thought, pretty silly.

"See how easy it is?" Lindsey asked. "Anytime you hear the word 'heart,' you just go like this." She traced a heart in the air again.

"Wow, that looks way too complicated," Alex fibbed. "Now that I've seen it, I know I would just make a fool out of myself up there. And I am trying very hard not to commit myself to too many activities anymore. But I promise that I will be cheering you on backstage."

"Aw, it's not that complicated," Lindsey protested.

"If I can do it, you can do it!" Charlotte said, as she bumped into Rosa.

Alex glanced at the clock on Emily's nightstand. Four o'clock. She'd almost forgotten.

"Sorry, I have to get to Ava's game," she said, grabbing her backpack. "But you guys look great!"

Alex hurried out of the room, relieved to be spared from joining the dance routine.

Sometimes having a twin sister came in handy!

Belle Payton isn't a twin herself, but she does have twin brothers! She spent much of her childhood in the bleachers reading—er, cheering them on—at their football games. Though she left the South long ago to become a children's book editor in New York City, Belle still drinks approximately a gallon of sweet tea a week and loves treating her friends to her famous homemade mac-and-cheese. Belle is the author of many books for children and tweens, and is currently having a blast writing two sides to each It Takes Two story.